ASCENDING

KENNA MCKINNON

This novella is dedicated to:
My sister, Judith Holmes
Angus
and my daughter, Diane Wild
All the dearest of the dear.

1

Bracing her wiry biceps, Scarlett Kane hoisted her three-year-old son into his booster seat at the kitchen table. The young woman's husband, Michael, slammed the front door as he stormed out of their rented yellow house. Her face twisted in dismay, realizing that once again she had failed as a wife and her husband had staged a fight to leave. Little Troy looked up at her with wide blue eyes. Upset with her husband, she was rough putting him into his seat. He squirmed.

"Hurting me, mommy." The child sucked on his fist and whimpered.

"Sorry, Troy. Your daddy's gone. He left us alone again."

"Daddy bad?"

Scarlett sighed. "If you're not careful, you'll grow up that way, too. All men do. Eventually."

"Daddy hurt you, Mommy?" His cornflower blue eyes searched hers. He picked up a spoon. The floor beneath the table shone. A tricycle was parked in one corner where their cat played with a ball that belonged to Troy.

She waggled a finger at her son. "Don't say that, dear."

"I want to hurt Daddy," Troy asserted, sticking out his small chest. "He hurt you, mom."

"When you grow up, you will look after the house," Scarlett suggested, changing the subject.

The boy frowned. "I don't want to grow up, Mommy. Can I be a baby again?"

"No, dear. It doesn't work that way."

"I don't want to grow up."

* * *

One Friday on June 11, 1971, Michael Joseph Kane used all his savings to buy a gorgeous demo motorcycle. One of the best days of his life – he was on top of the world. Drops of water glinted on chrome and steel as the orange Honda CB-750 Four K1 bike came to a guttural stop in front of his house.

Michael first took the baffles out for a meatier sound, but otherwise he didn't open the engine. He pushed the choke lever and stomped on the kick starter, and here came this motorcycle floating down the street as he hit the gears. The light was green for him and the Honda screamed through the intersection.

His wife, Scarlett Kane, pushed a lock of her rusty brown hair from her forehead and cradled Troy's curly head in one hand as she pulled shut the bay window. Rocker Patch, their marmalade cat, thumped to the floor.

Rocker had always been Michael's cat. Michael had named him after a motorcycle accessory. Scarlett was fond of Rocker Patch but the cat avoided her in favor of Michael and Troy. Max, her blue-feathered parakeet, twittered from his cage in the living room, and Angus, Scarlett's grey Scottie mix terrier, woofed.

Scarlett flung open the Harvest Gold refrigerator door and placed a dish of mac and cheese in the big old microwave oven someone had given them, which loomed like a giant alien on the counter next to the sink. In two minutes, the timer dinged and she took out the lunch, placed it in front of Troy with a plastic spoon and a glass of milk. She adjusted his blue bib.

"Eat," she commanded.

Obedient, the child spooned pasta into his mouth. His blue eyes sought her bright azure gaze. Macaroni and cheese formed a messy glob around his dish as he ate, some of it landing on the sparkling tile floor under the table. Some ran down the wall beside him. Scarlett groaned.

"Can't you be more careful?" She mopped at the mess.

"Finished?" she asked. He nodded.

"All gone." He made circles with his spoon on the wet surface of the table.

Scarlett whipped the bib off his neck and lifted him from the booster seat. "Stop that."

"Your father's coming back soon," she continued, but she knew it was a lie. Michael would not return for hours. Rain pelted against the window. Her parakeet Max trilled in his cage in the next room. She usually left the television on for the bird because he liked the sound. She strode into the mahogany paneled living room and turned off the set. Max squawked.

"Time for your nap," she said to the small child.

"Not sleepy. Don't want a nap. I'm a big boy."

Scarlett put him down and led him to his bedroom, where red curtains and a red cotton spread contrasted with the black and white modern wallpaper behind his bed. On the opposite wall, a mural of a clown had been painted. A red wooden toybox and white dresser stood against the other wall between two low windows. Toys and coloring books littered the carpeted floor.

He stumbled to his bed in his jeans and short tee-shirt. The cat followed.

"True," she murmured. "You're probably too old for a nap. Just rest, Troy. Close your eyes for a few minutes and leave me alone."

"Sleep with me, mom?"

Scarlett placed her lips on his damp forehead. "You've been playing too hard this morning, dear. You're sweating, and your hands are sticky from lunch." She wiped his hands with her apron and sighed again.

"Can I have a glass of water, puh-leeze, mom?"

"Okay." Scarlett tiptoed into the hallway, wet a washcloth from the bathroom faucet then let the water run until it was cold. She reached up and took down a paper cup from the dispenser on the wall. She filled the cup and slipped back into the child's room. He was watching her with wide blue eyes. His curly blond hair fanned out over the brightly patterned pillowcase as he pulled the sheet up over his chest.

He drank thirstily. She washed his hands and face. He pushed her hands away and grinned at her. "I love you, mom."

"I love you, too, Troy."

"Do we love daddy, mom?"

Scarlett flushed. "Yes, of course, dear."

"I love Angus, too. He's a good dog." She looked around but decided Angus must be in the yard outside. Max sang. Little Troy rubbed his eyes and yawned.

"You're sleepy," she whispered. "Rest now."

"Okay, mommy."

Later that evening, after lunch, after dinner, after bedtime for Troy, his mother sipped on a cup of Red Rose tea in her kitchen with Nancy Clarke, her next-door neighbor. The women had become close friends as well as neighbors and depended on one another rather than their fickle husbands. Amazingly, Nancy's trucker husband, Jack, was home tonight and minded their son Scott in his own unique fashion, a bottle of beer in one hand and the sports page in the other.

They hugged to say goodnight. Nancy slipped out the back door to her grey stucco house across the street.

Scarlett knew she could trust Nancy with not only her life but her child's life.

2

On April 4, 1968, years before fathers were allowed to attend the delivery of their own child, Scarlett Kane remembered the pain first and the nurses around her, then the doctor standing at her feet guiding the birth. She regretted that her handsome blond husband, Michael, was not present in the room. The baby gushed out of her womb, releasing the pressure. The baby cried.

The doctor smiled and held him up. "It's a boy!"

The mother's azure eyes danced. Her husband would be overjoyed. Michael wanted a boy so much. She had to have a boy. She had validated herself and him by giving birth to a son. Her chest swelled and she took large, deep, savoring breaths. A nurse allowed Scarlett to hold her son before the doctor whisked him off to see Michael in the waiting room.

They called the baby Troy Michael Kane. Michael agreed to calling their child after the old tales of the Trojan war, and the alleged discovery of Troy by the German adventurer and archeologist Heinrich Schliemann. "Let's not call him Heinrich Schliemann," Michael laughed. "Kane is too Irish for that and Schliemann too shady. Troy Michael it is. He'll be a hero."

His wife murmured from her hospital bed, "The name also means 'foot soldier' in Irish Gaelic."

"Fitting," Michael commented and flexed his biceps. "My son the warrior."

Scarlett's mother had been a fan of *Gone with the Wind* and Scarlett loved being named after the strong female character in the book and epic movie. She hoped her son would also love his historic nomenclature.

At birth the boy weighed eight pounds fifteen ounces and was twenty-one inches long. His mother kept a shock of his pale hair in a blue baby book, which was a gift; later recorded his height, weight, first adventures, and vaccinations at various times of his childhood.

Troy had eczema shortly after birth, on the left side of his face, unsightly at first, and their close friends said, "Aww, so cute," when they first saw him, then stopped when he turned his little face to the other side and they were shocked at the red mottle. Scarlett's stomach fell at their reaction but she and Michael were so proud and delighted with their new baby boy.

She applied ointments, wheeled him in his baby carriage to expose him to filtered sunlight and fresh air every morning, down the long tree-lined streets of their neighborhood, past the gossiping neighbors on their front stoops, and the eczema eventually healed.

Michael washed the baby's clothes in a laundromat because they lived in a cheap rented house with no laundry facilities. The husband used a lot of bleach on the baby's clothes and washed out all the vibrant colors. Scarlett thought the bleach contributed to the eczema.

Her husband used lots of very hot water and bleach because he was a clean freak, which helped when his wife needed assistance with chores. He vacuumed all the carpets weekly and tidied their belongings in drawers and closets, which were always neat and well organized thanks to him. Michael was very active and useful.

His son remembered him forever although Troy was barely three when Michael Joseph Kane died in a horrific fiery motorcycle crash over the side of a bridge and shattered his helmet on a light standard below. His son remembered fondly and with some puzzlement the circus and the swimming pools that his father took him to when he was small, before his father didn't ever come back again into his life. Barely three years old at the time, he remembered his mother crying when she left him with Scott's mother one morning and his father did not come back as he usually eventually did.

After death. What is that? Troy didn't understand, such a little boy he was, and waited at the window many days for his father to come home again.

Scarlett really didn't understand, either, and the guilt overwhelmed her. Her last memory of Michael was the senseless fight, the door slamming, and the sound of the Honda bike as it roared away, down the street and to eternity.

3

The nebulous voice on the other end of the phone could have been a woman's or it could have been a man's – in 1971, there was no call display. The number and the voice's identity remained a mystery. "Is Michael Kane there?"

"We buried him today." Scarlett Kane's tone was flat as she spoke into the receiver.

"Oh, really?" The disguised voice gloated.

"Hang up," urged her sister, and Scarlett settled the instrument onto its cradle.

Often thereafter when the clunky green wall phone rang, there was no one on the other end, or an amorphous voice asked for Michael Kane; for the first time the day of his funeral when she and the motley funeral entourage returned to the yellow rented house they had shared. It happened again, more often in the evening. Only once in the middle of the night.

Someone in the neighborhood bought a motorcycle and slammed its cacophony down the length of the street two blocks from her home. The engine's intermittent bellow cruised the residential area where Scarlett lived, but she never saw the rider and she knew only from the smoky belch of the machine up and down the same streets after dusk that it had to be a resident of her neighborhood joyriding their fantasy into her darkest fears.

The ghostly sounds began with a scratching behind the walls and a hollow tick-tock by one of the windows in three-year-old Troy Kane's bedroom. His curtains didn't quite reach together in the center and the boy complained of a light in his room. The child awakened many a night with fantasies of blue moonbeams floating on dust motes at midnight illuminated by intermittent bursts of beams from an invisible torch.

"Mommy," Troy confided to his mother in hushed tones while they were still in the yellow house, as the small robot he was constructing with his building blocks took shape, "A man's outside my room at night. He shines a light in my room."

Scarlett's heart was small and shrunken within her, afraid of what she may find or have to do to protect the boy, but she checked that afternoon for footprints on the west side of the house, and sure enough, there were imprints in the soft earth by the honeysuckle bush in front of the window.

She consulted her Ouija board and crystals for omens rather than call the police right away, but found nothing helpful. Her late husband Michael's workshop in the attached garage yielded a plethora of tools, some bills and receipts stuffed into an old tobacco can, but no clue as to who might want to hurt his family after the tragic motorbike accident that left her a single mom and many unanswered questions about secrets in the marriage.

Scarlett and her son continued to live in the rented house. Michael's company paid her a substantial amount of life insurance after his death, but Scarlett feared at first that it wouldn't go far enough to support a new home, even with the low cost of real estate in 1971. She invested the money and lived frugally on the interest for three more years until an older house in the working-class community of Calder was too much of a bargain to turn down.

In February of 1974, Scarlett bought a frame flat-roofed, two-bedroom dwelling with a back porch and partially finished basement, in the Calder area near the old Canadian National Railroad tracks. The fence leaned like a drunken soldier on a prostitute's arm but the building appeared newly painted, blue as Scarlett's eyes, and was neat and clean inside. Troy, now six years old, transferred to Calder School and started Grade One. They left behind them her friend Nancy Clarke and her son Troy's best friend, Scott.

"I hate goodbyes," Scarlett said to her friend after the two hired movers drove away with their sparse furniture and boxes in the rented truck. Scarlett's dog Angus whined underfoot. She planned to take Rocker Patch with her, but left the dog and her parakeet with Nancy, promising to take them back someday.

She knew that she wouldn't be back – knew in her bones that this was a break from the past and the game had changed. An abused wife, she would love herself, be herself, and shine despite those who never believed she could.

"You don't have to say goodbye," Nancy replied and scratched Angus under the chin. He thrust his wet muzzle into her hand and woofed softly.

"I'll always have a bit of you and Troy with me. As well as Michael." She wiped a tear from the corner of her eye. "Don't worry. I'll take good care of Angus and Max as though they were my own. It's not that I have anything else to do all day, with Jack away on the road all month. We don't have pets of our own, so Angus will fit right in, won't you, boy?"

The dog gazed up at Scarlett then at Nancy, as though he knew he had a new forever home with familiar friends. His loving brown eyes were shielded by grey brows. His tags sparkled from the red collar. He wagged his tail and whined.

"He loves you, mom," Troy's friend Scott commented,

tipping the parakeet Max in his steel blue cage, and poured seed into the cup. Max squawked.

Scarlett drew six-year-old Troy to her in a careful hug. She reached out a hand to her friend and neighbor. "Thank you so much."

"'Bye Scott. 'Bye Mrs. Clarke." Troy ran to Scott and punched him on the arm. "I'll miss you."

Michael and Scarlett Kane had lived in the rented house since before Troy was born. Her husband dead now for three years since that horrible morning when his motorbike crashed and burned under the overpass, Scarlett knew it was time to move on.

"This is a big step for us," she said.

Nancy held her friend's hand a moment longer. She reminded her, "If you fall, you'll rise up even stronger because you're a survivor. You're not a victim. You're in control of your life, sweetheart. There's nothing you can't achieve."

"Life has knocked me down a few times," Scarlett admitted. "I think I've learned in these last three years, though, to make lemon drop cocktails out of lemons. With a lemon twist! And then I learned to stop drinking after all that fun!"

Nancy laughed. "Atta girl! I was worried about your drinking after Michael died. You go get 'em, honey."

They left in the white Chevette that had replaced the Austin Healey Sprite. Angus howled when he saw them go, tried to follow, wagging his tail and straining at his leash, and Max chattered. They drove away and looked back only once, cementing the vision of their friends in their memories until after many years had passed. Awaited by a new home, new friends and neighbors, a new life, and a new school for Troy, her gut felt empty and aching, but there was also excitement.

4

———

Michael and Scarlett married on May 20, 1965. On a rainy day in June he and Scarlett returned from their Banff honeymoon. That morning they moved into their new home. Their meager furnishings had been delivered. As they had just arrived, their Sprite's engine was not yet cold.

The orange tabby kitten had used up his nine lives cohabiting with a feral brood on the streets and lived on borrowed days when Michael Kane first found him, huddled wet, dripping, and cold beneath their engine mount.

They didn't know the pedigree, age, nor name of the kitten that emerged squealing and bouncing stiff-legged from under the relative warmth of the car but like the infamous bad penny he hung around the young mechanical expert until Michael convinced his wife to adopt the handsome little cat.

At the time, Michael's new bride owned a grey Scottish terrier / bichon / poodle mix dog she called Angus, as well as a parakeet named Max.

"All right, if he doesn't bother Angus," Scarlett said. Her dog lay on his belly, feet splayed, at the edge of the carpet in the hallway. His tail thumped when he saw the kitten, which wasn't so sure about making friends with a dog.

Shortly after their wedding on the long weekend in May, they moved into the yellow house near the Municipal Airport close to downtown as their first home together. The landlord didn't care how many pets they had so long as they kept up the rent and the rather large damage deposit to cover any damages or ruined carpets.

Angus woofed, stared, and shook himself as the stray cat crept sniffing around the perimeters of the living room and kitchen, into the open doors of one of the three bedrooms then shot under a double bed as though squirted from a mustard bottle.

"Hello, little tiger," Michael coaxed as he tried to persuade the kitten to come out from under the bed. "What do kittens eat?" he asked his bride and Scarlett shrugged. She was a dog person. Definitely not a cat person. But she humored her new husband and Angus didn't seem to mind the intruder. Rather, he tried to make friends with his new roommate, snuffling under the bed skirts to get a good smell of the kitten, who would have nothing of it. Scarlett had to smile at Angus's antics.

"What should we call him?" she asked as she opened a tin of sardines and shoved it under the bed.

"That's it," coaxed Michael. He pushed the sardines as far as they would slide in the direction of the kitten, who hissed and retreated further. Tail wagging, Angus woofed softly as he pushed his nose under the bed. The kitten hissed again.

"Spark Plug," declared Michael, crawling on all fours under the blue satin quilt at the foot of the bed.

"You can't call him Spark Plug," his wife objected, keeping a firm grip on the dog's harness. Angus looked bored. She popped a milk bone from an emptied cookie canister on the dresser, and he drooled over it a bit then attempted to bury it beneath a scatter rug. Scarlett took Angus by the collar to lead him out of the room. She closed the door and could see his nose and paws scrabbling at the patch of light under it.

"Why not? Gotcha!" Michael exclaimed and dragged the hissing and biting little ball of orange fluff from under the bedding, covered with bits of sardine.

On her knees, Scarlett retrieved the tin and the rest of the fish. "Ugh. Nasty little thing."

"I know you don't know much about cats," he muttered. "That doesn't mean you can't learn to love them."

"What if it doesn't get along with Angus in the long run? Or Max? What if it eats Max? Max isn't used to cats or the outside world. He's brand new from the bird shop." In the background her parakeet tweeted and tried to mimic the frantic meowls of the kitten.

"Trust me," Michael grunted and slipped the kitten under his shirt, stroking the tiny tiger-striped animal until it relaxed. "Why not call him Spark Plug? I just cleaned the carburetor and plugs of the Sprite last month. Why not Sparky?"

"No."

"Then something fancy. I've got a liking for bikes. How about…" He consulted a memory in his clever mind of a sales brochure for Honda motorcycles he was looking at the day before. "Rocker Patch," he concluded. "We could call him Rocker or Patch for short."

"What's that mean?" asked Scarlett.

He explained, "A Rocker Patch is a badge worn by a member of a motorcycle club to identify the club and sometimes the location. A family-oriented motorcycle club usually only has a one-piece badge or "rocker." The outlaw clubs have three-piece badges. It's also known as 'flying your colors' from the military regimental colors."

"I don't like it," the young wife stated. "I don't like the idea of you ever getting a motorcycle, either, or belonging to a gang."

"Not a gang. A club," he insisted. "but drop the topic."

"You're not a safe driver."

Their red Sprite sportscar had a new dent in the front corner from his latest fender bender accident. He knew she thought he was a reckless driver, but to her credit, and perhaps her personal safety, she never mentioned it to him when he was at the wheel.

There had been that unfortunate incident when he fell into a rage when questioned. Never again, Scarlett thought, frightened and somewhat awed by his violence like a sudden summer storm from Almighty Thor. No ark nor drawbridge to raise were available to her to protect herself from the elemental fury of her husband's whimsical moods. So, she kept quiet and as her mother said, remained from childhood to marriage a "good" girl.

"Oh, yes, I see," she said now, as Michael drew his left arm around her shoulders and hugged her closer. "It's a club."

He set the kitten on a pile of sheets. "We'll call him Rocker Patch. I kind of like it. It has a biker connection. He's kind of a cool kitty."

"Did you have a cat when you were a boy?"

He grinned. "Yeah. He'll be good luck for us."

"It might be hard to get someone to look after him as well as Angus and Max when we go on holidays. Do you think we should split visits between our families for Christmas and Thanksgiving?" she asked. "I haven't met your parents yet, but they're closer than mine are in Fort St. John, aren't they? I thought your family lived closer. With a houseful of pets for us to think about, maybe they'd come here in October?"

She opened the door and let her dog into the room again. Angus whined and thumped his tail on the rug, eager to make friends. The kitten jumped down from his nest on the sheets and crept closer to touch noses. "Oh, look! Isn't that cute!"

The parakeet sang. Their home seemed complete.

"I don't see my family," he said. "That's why you've never met them. That's why we couldn't have a big family wedding. You knew that."

"I thought it was because my parents hesitated at first to attend. But they finally did. Surprise."

"No. I didn't want any of my relatives or family at our wedding. Your parents, sisters, and the couple we got as witnesses were enough. I think our friends were disappointed, though."

She touched him on the shoulder. "You got your wish, then. It doesn't matter to me. I was so pleased my parents drove down to be here that nothing else mattered."

"They even got us a gift. We didn't expect that."

For two young people who had never known a lot of love, it was an inauspicious start to their marriage. But they didn't know that. They were young and thoughtless, and good communication wasn't part of their natures, nor did they expect it. Neither one of them had a lot of love to give, either, but both craved the closeness and the escape from loneliness.

"I'd like to meet your mother," she said.

"Maybe someday."

"If you and I hadn't met at your company, we might not have met at all or dated for six months before we bought the pink champagne that loosened your tongue to propose to me. We might never have married."

He snorted. "It's all chance."

"No, it isn't," she objected. "It is not, Michael Joseph Kane."

Picking up Rocker, he unfolded the soft warm kitten into her palm. "I love you."

"I love you, too." She pressed her cheek onto the fuzzy orange feline's body. It snuggled and began to purr. Angus thrust his wet muzzle into her other hand. She rubbed the crinkly grey skull between his alert ears. "Angus is such a good boy. I think he'll be good with the kitten, don't you?"

Michael glanced at the grey Scottie with the red bandana around its neck, the warm brown eyes adoring his wife, and tail thumping gently. Michael's voice sounded unlike himself as he murmured in deeper tones, "Yes. Now let's go into the other room. I want us to try out our new recliner. What a great gift!"

She snuggled into his arms soft as the kitten. "Will it fit two?" she asked.

"Oh, yes," he said. Max sang as he kissed her.

5

Scarlett felt that there were two sides to her husband – anger and love– and she never knew which would surface. After the times he became restless, the comforting Michael took his place; he stopped pacing and his face softened almost as though he were another man. At those times she loved him most. They almost made up for the outbursts of rage and the isolation she experienced when he left for entire nights at a time. This was compounded by an initial depression after Troy was born that later would be diagnosed as post-partum in character but, she was sure, was due to extrinsic factors. The depression didn't completely dissipate and would later morph into something more sinister.

Often, she was left alone at night with the baby. In the pale orange wash of evening after work, Michael would stage another argument that sent him out of their home for hours. "When will you be back, Mike?"

He didn't answer, his brows lowering as he glanced back at her with that electric blue gaze that stopped her spirit.

He turned the overhead light on in the early morning and woke her before he left for work. At those times, awakened by a bright light at three o'clock in the morning, she thought that she would rather die than endure another day.

"The light hurts my eyes," she complained but did not question the timing nor the long absences. She was afraid to arouse his brutality. But the thought of leaving did not occur to her. She had no idea of how she would survive without him.

"No, it doesn't," he growled. "Your eyes are closed. The light doesn't shine through your eyelids. Go back to sleep."

"It does," she replied but obediently suffered and he turned off the light.

"Darling!" Michael exclaimed the next morning. "I've made you a Hoagie for breakfast."

"Your specialty," she remarked as the baby sucked at her breasts. Her husband was intermittently loving, and what her mother called "a good provider" as a draftsman at a local oil company, Coral Bay Oil & Gas Inc. It was a job that paid adequately if not well and a good match to his skills. He loved his job.

Scarlett had worked as a file clerk for Coral Bay before their marriage. After their wedding, she quit work and hoped to be a "kept woman", a term which made her smile and endeared her husband to her more than his presence sometimes. Scarlett was not well educated beyond high school, but Michael had attended university for two years in an engineering program and she felt he was more intelligent than she. She struggled to keep up, read voraciously, and he sometimes remarked that she was "bright" and he was "clever". She didn't know the difference, but felt mollified in her role as homemaker.

They planned another child, hoping for a girl to complete a million-dollar family. They would call her Shannon because Scarlett's grandmother had married a Shannon.

Not to be, this little pink bundle of promise did not materialize nor take shape through many months of failure. Michael, rough and virile in lovemaking, blamed his wife. He withdrew from the marriage bed and his erections were infrequent.

"I feel like a stud," he complained as the cat perched on the windowsill and watched them. "I'm only performing to make another baby. Is that all you want of me?"

Their daughter remained a pink fantasy in their minds, and the rare times that Michael grew thoughtful and caring, were the times she cherished as perhaps a promise of what was to become of the marriage and maybe the soft cradle of another maternity.

Rather than pay for his wife to go to a dentist, he urged her to have her teeth extracted and she thought this was only one way to make her more like his mother, though she didn't know his family at all.

Michael grew ever more distant and uncaring, and stayed away for more nights in a row than he was with her. Sometimes before he left, before the fights, he was more loving, inexplicably so, exhausting Scarlett with the duplicity of his persona. She hated and feared her husband, yet listened for the sound of their car as it turned the corner to come home. She knew the sound of the engine without seeing the vehicle. That's how very much her soul strained to unite with his. She was afraid he would die in a fiery crash with their new Chevette. She knew how reckless he was.

Michael, however, finally agreed to marriage counseling and she thought it was in desperation that he agreed, because he was less of a man in bed than he should be at twenty-five years of age, although he said he was too old to enjoy a night of lovemaking.

Scarlett called Family Services one afternoon after consulting with Michael. "We'll provide counseling within your budget," the receptionist assured her. "We have a sliding scale.

We don't turn anyone away. I think Dr. Tumulak is free next week."

With Michael asleep in the next room, she made an appointment for the following Tuesday with a social worker, Lawrence Tumulak, PhD, for the two of them to see him to perhaps save their marriage. In Scarlett's mind, all hinged on Lawrence to fix them.

"He's judgmental though he says he's not," declared Michael after their first appointment, but he agreed to return. "I like the little guy, though."

In a few weeks, Lawrence began to see them separately. He knew nothing of Scarlett's childhood and didn't ask. Her sessions revolved around her husband. She commented one day that her mother had been the strong person in their family. Lawrence frowned and his face twisted. Scarlett realized that these two men feared and hated strong women.

"I wish I had him in my pocket so I could consult him when I need him," Michael exclaimed a couple of months later. "I love him. I cried and he just held me."

Lawrence leaned across his enormous teak desk to Scarlett in one of their private sessions. "It scared me. Your husband at the core is a woman. I was about to say he's schizophrenic, because of the personality and mood shifts. But he's his mother."

"I don't know his mother." Scarlett frowned. "Isn't it Freudian to blame the mother?"

"Freud was right in every respect," replied the therapist. "Every woman he meets becomes his mother. You castrated your father and you're trying to castrate your husband. It's your fault he hits you. You're provoking him. Do you enjoy it?"

"No," she said, and was very careful not to provoke Michael into another rage. It worked for a time, but she became withdrawn and more depressed. As her mother said, she was a "good girl."

"You're cured," declared Lawrence to Scarlett after a year. "You were two unloving people and I made a new personality for you. You don't have to come back. But I want to see your husband." Then her real illness began.

* * *

His body was soiled and broken at the bottom of the overpass and his motorcycle helmet cracked in many pieces from the force of the impact of his head on the light standard. She consulted Lawrence one more time.

"It wasn't suicide," the therapist said in response to her suggestion, showing her his appointment book with multiple entries for Michael over the next six months. "He would have called me and canceled his appointments."

No. He wouldn't have, you dunce. You court jester with a phony degree. The therapist fixed their marriage, all right. He fixed Scarlett, all right. He sure fixed Michael. They trusted him and he destroyed them both.

6

Scarlett survived but her depression deepened and her soul split in two like Michael's heart. She both rejected and clung to the son who was her greatest treasure. She suspected he needed a new father, but she was afraid of another romantic relationship though opportunities presented themselves. She doubted that any force on earth would make her whole again. Especially another man.

Then came Michael's ghost, riding the midnight air on hot wheels of fire and memory, descant to a melody of rip tide and fury. He had never lain quiet in his grave. The very walls moved with the rage that remained and the lights of reason dimmed and flickered in Scarlett's brain.

She had insurance money, carefully budgeted, she had memories of a kind and loving Michael that eventually superseded the memory of abuse. But the house where she lived and dreamed was a cubicle of unease. Michael's soul did not rest.

Indeed, his soul did not rest at all. Into the long evenings when she planned the weeks to come and listened for sounds in her son's room, she stitched from the fabric of her former being a new stubbornness. First, she had to demolish the lie that had been created by the Freudian therapist, and the misshapen world of his sexuality, and her family's dysfunction, and she had to mold the world she would make for herself and her child.

The Mother Goose Hotel was just down the street from the rented house she had shared with Michael. As a variety of babysitters came and went, Scarlett sat at the bar and drank with strange men. Sometimes she took them home.

Troy suffered with neglect. "I'm hungry, mom," he said, as she lay in bed at four o'clock in the afternoon, unconscious from drink the night before. Or ...

Her neighbor Nancy consoled her with trite phrases. "You're a good woman. A kind person. There's nothing you wouldn't do for a friend. I know you're grieving for Michael. But what about the child?"

Scarlett was confused and split. Slowly the pieces flowed back together when she discovered that she could buy a bottle of cherry whiskey in the liquor store and drink it at home by herself. She didn't need to go to a bar! She could drink privately and secretively, and she did.

"Pull yourself together, Scarlett," Nancy said, hugging the small boy, who looked at his mother with wide blue eyes full of hurt and confusion. "Look what I found in *The Journal*."

A newspaper clipping with Classified Ads gave the name in small letters of AA (Alcoholics Anonymous) and a number to call. Brian.

Scarlett, desperate and sick, called the number two days later.

"I'll take care of Troy while you go to the meeting," declared Nancy, her hazel eyes full of tears. "I've never seen you like this. Michael's spirit would be distressed to know how you've fallen, my friend."

"Get yourself to a meeting and put the plug in the jug," said Brian when she called him. "Where do you live? I'll be right over. There's a North End meeting in the Anglican church just ten blocks from you. Coffee, fellowship, a new life. Hang in there, dear."

She sat at the table with a group of older smoking men and two women, and discovered a new life, as Brian had said. Alcoholics Anonymous has changed exponentially since the 1970s, but at that time, Scarlett found it not suited for a young woman – however, she hung in there, and was glad for it.

The smoke hung heavy in the room. A large battered tin pot dispensed cup after cup of hot black coffee.

"My name is Scarlett and I'm an alcoholic."

It was the most difficult thing she had ever said, and the most freeing.

"Hello, Scarlett." A chorus of friendly voices and friendly smiles greeted her. She was asked to speak and she cried.

She was home. After six months, she relapsed and drank. "Put the plug in the jug," Brian said. For another two weeks she was sober. Then she "got it."

Scarlett rejoiced in her newfound health and for two more years accepted the tokens she had earned in AA and did not drink.

Three years after Michael's death, she took the insurance money and her son and moved to a new neighborhood. The geographical cure, her acquaintances and friends at Alcoholics Anonymous declared. She did not return to the group but forged for herself a more determined personality. At her last meeting there she sang, "I've Been a Wild Rover for many a year..."

Her friends laughed and clapped, gave her cake and coffee, and she began a new existence with her son that was free and independent, yet not devoid of problems or the old hauntings that rang her phone at odd times in the evenings, scratched at the walls in Troy's room, and shone lights into the recesses of her homes both old and new.

The drinking seemed to be connected to a mental health problem caused by trauma. Perhaps the therapist Lawrence Tumulak should have addressed the trauma, but he did not, and Scarlett forged ahead just the same, from a depression born of hormones and extrinsic forces. Like a wet moldy blanket, it covered her brain, and like a strong woman, she threw it off.

More than herself, the beneficiary was her son Troy, who was now six years old and ready for a new home in Calder, the "geographic cure", and a mother who truly cared about herself and him.

"Children are very resilient," Nancy commented, not knowing of the darkness in a young life that was not yet addressed.

7

The clockworks Michael constructed and the unfinished engines in his garage workshop ticked by themselves for weeks after his death, then were silent. In 1974, his wife packed them up and brought them with her, their son, and the cat to their new home in Calder.

Troy had bonded with Rocker more than with Angus, in any case, and the dog went to a good home. Two more breaks with the past, Scarlett said to Nancy, and Nancy agreed it was a good thing when she accepted the dog and bird into her little grey stucco house by the Municipal Airport. Rocker prowled and meowled for a few days, searching for Angus, and the house seemed silent without Max's constant singing. But Scarlett felt she had made the right decision.

"It's time to move on," her friend said, hugging her. "The past is done with, and the pets were more Michael's than yours, in any case."

"That's right," Scarlett said, not surprised but hurt. "How did you know?"

"We were neighbors and friends, remember?"

"Sometimes I think you were a better friend to Michael."

"No," Nancy expostulated. "What makes you think that?"

"We had some great times together, didn't we, the three of us?"

Nancy's mouth twisted crookedly. "Well, my Jack was never here. What you get for marrying a trucker."

"Take good care of my pets, please." Angus whined and put his wet muzzle into Scarlett's outstretched hand. She scratched behind his ears. He shook his head and trotted over to Nancy. "See? He likes you better."

"He'll be a good companion for Scott. Scott will miss Troy so much, and I'll miss you. We'll have to keep in touch."

"Of course." But Scarlett knew her life now would not account for old friends nor former pets.

* * *

The house of Kane, it seemed, was cursed. Michael's mistress, or one of them, undoubtedly made the calls after her paramour's death, or arranged for them, and the lights at night into wee Troy's room? Not harmless but something from the dark side that his father had been involved with, drugs or alcohol-running to underage drinkers, or packages of weed hidden in public parks at night, in view of Michael's accomplices.

The phone rang and a disguised voice asked for Michael. "Is Michael Kane there?" Sometimes she thought the voice was a familiar one. She knew the calls came because he still rode the night streets and avenues of the city even though dead. In her dreams, she heard the wild tumble of his bike and saw the bloodied skull.

Michael didn't die in the cold dark rain that night on the cold dark slippery road and the bike out of control and he fighting it and then over the side into the post with the back of his head all broken open and his brains spilling out. His blackened soul would live until she said, "Rest in Peace."

She could not do that. She couldn't let go.

She loved him too much. It might have been love that clung to his memory and now the haunting. It might have been fear of the ghosts of memories in their lives – both were equally strong and equally valid. She didn't know.

The little clockwork machines he had made, the engines and the black iron industrial model railroads, the all-consuming hobbies that insulated him from her, she hated them and loved them. She kept them.

Scarlett continued the work Michael had begun in the dark basement of her new house, building, casting spells, consulting horoscopes: All the time filled with panic born of a twisted fascination with the haunting of her soul and danger to the boy she loved but could not protect, nor could she protect herself.

It was a nightmare from which she could not awaken. She sometimes called the police about the phone calls, and once she called Lawrence again, but mostly she fought her lone battles herself, and Troy suffered.

She loved to tinker, too, and imagined their son's pleasure with his father's toys when he was older. Also, it was a piece of Michael she could not leave behind. The only place he had seemed to find any peace was in his workshop.

She had memories of interrupting him there with cans of cola and sandwiches, and a kiss. So seldom was her husband content at home, that these were moments she cherished.

8

"Oh, boy!" Troy exclaimed when he saw the movers waiting at their new house in Calder. "We're bringing my red curtains and dad's toolboxes. I can see them on top of the boxes."

"We wouldn't forget anything so important," his mother replied. "Now let's go have some new experiences!"

Shortly after they first moved into the "blue house" as Troy called their new home, Scarlett answered the back doorbell and discovered three of her female neighbors perched on her grey back landing. Startled and pleased, Scarlett accepted a tuna casserole and an equally warm welcome, along with a pan of home baked brownies.

Each new friend had small children who went to Calder School, except for the also widowed Leela Balakrishnan from southern India, whose daughter and son attended the Catholic school, St. Edmund, at the end of the block. Penny and James Cardinal with their four young daughters and a son, Stevie, lived across the street from the convenience store.

Karin Sivertsen and her husband Victor, who worked as a supervisor at the CN Walker railroad yard, lived in a pretty house near the road that ran by the train tracks. Their twin boys were a match for Troy in age and looks, both being yellow-haired, tall, but sturdy like their parents.

The four Cardinal girls ranged in age from nine to one year old. Stevie was a nice boy about Troy's age. Penny spent hours arranging the girls' thick black hair into braids and waves, and James Cardinal paraded proudly with his family every Sunday to the Foursquare Gospel Church nearby. Troy often begged to go with them because Stevie was his best friend, and Scarlett thought it might be a good idea. She hesitated because she thought she should also attend, but wasn't ready to do that.

"What do you think?" asked Leela to Scarlett over muffins and tea in her kitchen. "Troy's six now, almost old enough to take first communion."

Scarlett bit her lip. "Your kids are Catholic. I don't think Penny's church has the same beliefs. Troy is a strange boy, full of ghosts and whispers from his father's past, though he barely remembers my husband, just still lifes in his mind of Michael taking him to the circus once when he was barely three and his daddy crying in the middle of the clown acts because our marriage was broken, and swimming at Coronation Pool where Michael taught him to jump off the low board into his arms."

Leela jumped to her feet to check on the children playing in her backyard. She whispered over her shoulder, "Does Troy ever ask you for a new daddy? My little Paul and Daisy..."

"No," Scarlett replied. "He wants his daddy back. I don't think he ever understood that death is for keeps."

Her friend frowned as she returned to the tidy kitchen table. Spreading jam onto a date muffin, she poured more tea for Scarlett and settled against the high back of the brown Naugahyde and chrome chair. "My children loved their father very much, but it was so long ago in their minds and they were so unhappy with the many hospital visits, and they said goodbye so many times before the cancer finally got him.

"We considered returning to India, but their home is here. So is mine, really, though my parents and sisters are all in Mysore still. There's the matter of faith, too. When Joachim and I became betrothed, his parents were against the marriage because they were Catholic and my family were Hindu. My family did not like Catholics, either. They wanted to arrange a marriage for me with a boy from a good Indian family. I would have none of it."

Scarlett stirred honey into her tea. The spoon rang against the china cup. She pursed her lips. "So, what did you do?"

Leela laughed. "We eloped."

"Oh."

"Yes, for three or four months before the ceremony, we attended marriage preparation classes without the knowledge of our families. When the day came, we ran away with two good friends who were our witnesses, and we got married in the historic and beautiful St. Philomena church on Ashoka Road. One of the priests was a good friend of Joachim's from college who knew the situation, and he rather regretfully performed the ceremony. We had his blessing, though, and the blessing of the Church. That was important to my husband.

"By the time our parents found out, it was too late. They tried to annul it. But we had already taken a two-week honeymoon in Sri Lanka and I was pregnant with Daisy by the time we came home, though nobody knew that yet until a month later."

"How romantic," gushed Scarlett, putting out her cigarette in a pewter ashtray. "And how scary! Did Joachim's family have money?"

"They were very wealthy and my family were poor. That was another source of dissent."

"What did you do then?"

Leela smiled. "His parents first had me sign a paper that our children be raised Catholic, then they gave us a large sum of gold and cash to go to America. When we got here, we chose Canada. The rest you know. Joachim taught physics at the University of Alberta until his death." She drew slim bejeweled fingers over her face and frowned. Her mirth had faded. "Pancreatic cancer..."

There was silence in the room for a few moments as the two friends considered their losses. "It was years ago now. My children don't remember him well, and they would like a new daddy. It's hard. I can't replace such a good man."

"Of course not." Scarlett placed her pale hand over Leela's upturned fingers.

Both women shook their heads and smiled. They rose to their feet again to check on the children in the back yard. Troy, twelve-year-old Daisy, and ten-year-old Paul were building a fort with old boards, a hammer, and nails from a battered tin.

"Children, would you like some juice?" called Scarlett's friend and on hearing the enthusiastic Yesses, she placed five plastic drinking glasses on a silver tray and filled them with lemonade. Scarlett carried the tray to the yard, where she admired their construction skills.

The women decided to sit on plastic web lawn chairs near the play area in the grassy yard. Each chair was equipped with a cup holder. They sipped on cold drinks and enjoyed the lengthening rays of the afternoon sun on this pleasant autumn day.

Leela waggled her bare legs over the edge of the chair. "Plans?" she asked. Scarlett raised her rusty brown eyebrows.

"What plans? Plans for what?"

"Do you have any plans for the future, now that you're settled here in Calder and Troy is in school?"

Scarlett shook her head. "I don't make plans for the future. Too uncertain."

"Everyone has goals."

Scarlett shrugged. "That's different."

"Yes, you're probably right." Leela placed her drink in the cup holder. She folded her hands in her lap then unfolded them. She sighed.

"You know what I mean, Scarlett. We're drifting since our husbands died. You don't have a real job. Mine is part-time and temporary. We have children who are growing up without fathers. I go door-to-door for the Cross Cancer Institute and you arrange home parties for Candle Party Lite. I know you used to work outside the home at an oil company before Troy was born. You've told me that's where you met Michael.

"But now, Scarlett, we don't *do* anything. We get up in the morning, we get dressed, we look pretty for our friends and children, we visit with our neighbors or in my case, go to work for three afternoons a week. We care for our precious children, who will grow up without fathers, and leave us finally. We will grow old."

"I've thought of that." Scarlett glanced at the happy children, chattering and shouting as they constructed their playhouse fort.

9

Six-year-old Troy rushed over to his mother. "Mom, mom!"

"What, dear?" She brushed a blade of grass from his tawny hair. He was growing tall, like his dad, and his blond curly hair was getting darker, like hers.

"Paul says I can have a sleepover at his house tonight. Can I, please?"

Scarlett glanced at Leela, who smiled and shrugged. "Sure," Leela said. "That's fine with me."

"Puh-leeze, mom? It'll be fun!"

"It's lonely at night, just you and me, isn't it?" Scarlett asked her son softly. She drew a menthol cigarette from its package and lit a match. Troy hugged her.

"Yeah," he said.

"All right," she said. "Just this one night. Remember, it's school tomorrow."

"Paul goes to a different school than I do. He goes to *St. Edmund.*"

"I know. That's no problem. You'll go to Calder as usual, come home for lunch. I'll see you then."

"Gee, thanks, mom!" Troy rushed away to join Paul and Daisy at the side of the house. Sounds of hammering ceased.

"I know what you mean," Scarlett said to Leela, pouting smoke rings over her upturned head. She wore her wedding rings on the third finger of her right hand. The demure diamond caught the last sparkle of the setting sun.

Though the lawns were still green, a master painter had caught the myriad golds and reds of the sunset in the rich foliage that lined the mature boulevards. A jet plane streamed its trail over a vast expanse of azure, like Scarlett's eyes, etching a white exclamation mark on the blue chalkboard of sky.

"We owe it to ourselves, and to the children," Leela ventured, leaning closer to her friend. "But I can't bear to think of it."

"Me neither," Scarlett replied. "Another husband? But who?"

"There's someone at my church..." Leela smiled and winked. "But he is so old."

"Is he rich?"

Leela laughed. "I don't know."

"Is he handsome?" Scarlett grinned. She ground the cigarette under the heel of her sandal. It sizzled in the grass, now dewy in the dusk of yet another day ending.

"I think so." Her friend smiled back. "That guy at the convenience store, John Aguila. He likes you, I think. He's not rich. He's a little bit handsome, though, and he is a very good man."

Scarlett sobered. "No," she said. She pushed back her lawn chair, got to her feet, and stretched. She reached down and pinched the crushed cigarette between her index finger and thumb. "Where do I put this, Leela?"

"In the cup will do," her friend replied.

The children's fort stood deserted. They had run to the front of Leela's charming white house and were playing kick the can on the sidewalk. The two mothers sat on the front porch and watched them.

"You know, Leela?" Scarlett wrinkled her forehead. "Troy still sees lights in his room at night, after dark, mostly hears sounds before the flashes he describes. Maybe somebody is spying on us? Maybe somebody is after my son? I've always dismissed it as childish fantasy. I think I was afraid to find out – what or who it really is. Or that my son is crazy." She barked a short chuckle. "Or I am. What do you think?"

"Troy is not crazy," Leela said, folding her arms. "That I know. You are not crazy, either, but you better get a grip, Scarlett. You haven't told me this before. Does it have anything to do with the phone calls you get, still, after all these years?"

"I don't know. Do you think I should call the police again?"

Leela's brow wrinkled. "Definitely he might be making it up, missing his daddy so much, the trauma. You moved to get away from it?"

"No, it's not that," Scarlett objected. "I moved because I wanted a permanent home for my son and me. But yes, the phone calls continue. There's the constant sense of being spied on. My son's complaints of someone looking in his room at night with a flashlight, and scratching at the walls. Even now, when the curtains are so thick and drawn tightly over his window, he says he sees phantom lights in his room.

"I go in there when he calls out, but I never see anything. The police are worthless without anything concrete to go on. They dismiss my fears. I've tried calling them and a couple of times they came out. But nothing."

"You have to investigate further," Leela said. "In my role as a social worker when we first came to Canada, I saw many odd and disturbing events and met a few vicious and different kinds of people, as well as many good people like yourself."

She laid a gentle hand on Scarlett's shoulder. "Here, now, our children need us. Let's talk about this tomorrow, shall we?"

"I'll go home and get Troy's pajamas for tonight and clothes for tomorrow morning," Scarlett said. "Thanks for listening. I don't think there's anything to worry about. We haven't been hurt in the three years since Michael died, and there isn't anything that's going to hurt us now, I'm sure. It's just so – so odd that Troy would have the same delusions since his father died of someone trying to spy on him at night, time after time, and in two completely different neighborhoods over a span of several years.

"I feel angry with myself for not insisting that something be done sooner. I was a bad mom."

"No, you're a good mother," Leela objected. "Sometimes it feels safer to be in denial."

"I'm not in denial," snapped Scarlett, then she stopped and slapped her forehead. "I guess I am!"

The children still played kick the can, oblivious to the turn the conversation between their mothers had taken. Scarlett rose and slipped across the street to her own modest house, collected Troy's belongings, and bundled them against her chest as she trudged again to Leela's place.

"I'm going to sleep in his room tonight," she told her friend. "I'm going to see what happens. You know, the little guy has always slept alone."

"The Cardinals all sleep together. It's musical beds at their place," Leela said. She took the bundle of clothes. "It's their custom. They think it's cruel to let our children sleep alone."

The phone on her wall was ringing when Scarlett got home that night. She didn't answer it. She didn't sleep in Troy's room, either. She was afraid to.

10

Beside their new home in Calder sparkled a community skating rink and shack. Down the street from that, a convenience store sold chocolate bars in packs of four, menthol cigarettes, loaves of bread with so many preservatives that the loaf could serve as a cornerstone for a century and still be fresh, and milk often well past its expiration date, which Scarlett refused to buy.

Middle-aged and handsome, John Aguila owned the store. He had his eye on Scarlett from the first day she walked into the shop. She noted his naturally dark complexion and his Spanish aquiline nose, his abs under the cotton sweaters he wore, with just a hint of an adorable paunch, and the way his biceps bulged as he handled the heavy boxes in the back of the store. He was an interesting counterpoint to her blond deceased husband, but she wasn't interested in another man just the same.

Lonely, she did often stay to chat for a few minutes amidst the chirping of his budgies hung in a vintage bronze cage by the well stocked shelves.

"I had a parakeet named Max," she commented as John

busied himself wiping the counter. "The shop I bought him from said they could learn to talk like a parrot."

"Did you ever try?" John asked, smiling at her.

"No. It seemed too much trouble and by that time we had our little boy to keep me busy."

The shop owner stopped and put the cloth down. "I get away and close up the store for two months in the winter, so won't always be here to help. But while I'm here, I'm happy to help out if you ever need anything."

"What kind of things?"

"I could deliver bread and fresh milk to your house for a small extra charge for delivery, so you wouldn't have to come in so often with the boy to care for and everything. What do you think of that? I did it for the family who used to own your house. It's no trouble."

She agreed for the winter months, except for January and February, when the shopkeeper closed his store.

"They have to be fresh," she cautioned.

"For you? Of course," he replied. "I get new stock every Monday morning. I'll deliver on Monday afternoons. No big deal."

Scarlett scampered home, sure that she had just made inroads on an interesting new experience. Certainly, she still wasn't ready for another man in her life. At first, she wasn't positive that she even liked John Aguila; thought he was meddling. But as Leela said, it was pretty obvious that he liked her. Hmmm - like every recovering alcoholic, the scenario played out in Scarlett's head like a movie, and before she arrived back at her door, she was positive she wouldn't let him inside her house, even if he came to deliver milk and bread, or whatever. The card he had thrust into her hand before she left the store would go immediately into the trash.

Instead, she placed the card in the antique desk in her

living room, in the back with receipts and bills, and forgot about it until many months later.

John Aguila continued to cash her baby bonus cheques for her and gave Troy little treats. John thought Troy needed a daddy. Scarlett was determined that Troy needed her and no one else.

"Here you are, little man," he said. "Do you like oranges?"

John didn't know how wicked she was or how she hurt the ones who loved her, she thought. Nobody knew except Michael. It was a secret.

Within a couple of years, his persistence and Scarlett's close proximity and feminine nature resulted in a comfortable opposite gender relationship that would last a lifetime, but alas, John, no spark of desire for you was set alight in her breast or consummation to complete your longing!

That would forever belong to the man known as Michael Joseph Kane.

11

The night of Michael's death, the slim brown-haired woman who was his wife lay on her back in their double bed in the room with the purple walls and white goatskin rug, and stared at the shifting patterns on the ceiling. It was late; very late.

The rain had stopped and the clouds cleared to allow the moonlight to glint on the bottles that lined the dresser. She closed her eyes.

At five in the morning, Scarlett awakened to the chimes of the front doorbell. Stumbling, she threw on her robe and confronted the two uniformed officers at the door. "Mrs. Kane?"

"Yes?" Her heart sank at sight of the police officers, one tall, lanky, and grave, the other a small female who screwed up her eyes and twisted her mouth, prepared to deliver bad news. Scarlett knew. She grasped the door jamb.

"There's been an accident."

"Yes." Scarlett felt very calm. Air gushed into her ears, rendering her temporarily deaf, but her voice was firm though it echoed in her head.

"May we come in?"

Voicelessly, she moved to one side.

He had been a reckless driver. Always. She knew. Always. It was time. The proper meridian had coincided with the stars. In the middle of the night, her husband had been traveling too fast on slick streets over the Groat Road overpass on the way to the south side of Edmonton. The Honda CB-750 is a state-of-the art bike. A superbike, some would say, and the first of its kind, a trailblazer for bikes and a huge engine for the time. Michael had received forty-five minutes of instruction before he drove it out of the lot two days ago.

In 1971 a driver of a motorbike in Alberta didn't need a special licence other than their automobile driver's licence. That was to change, but too late for the hapless and reckless Michael, his family, and mistress.

The big engine had been too much for him to handle, his bike skid on the overpass on a wet street, the black mist in his face, his helmet crushed by the light standard he slammed with the back of his head at one hundred and forty kilometers per hour. Too fast, too soon, so young.

He was twenty-nine years old, three years older than Scarlett. He would always be young now – he would never grow old. What had he said about turning thirty? He preferred to be forever young.

Forever young. Her face was pale and her hands trembled. Still she did not weep.

"Yes," she said in reply to a query from the tall male police officer. "I'll come with you. Give me a minute to get dressed and call my neighbor. We have a son."

"Can we do anything to help, ma'am?" The female cop didn't meet her eyes.

"You can give me a ride home again," Scarlett said.

She had to identify the soiled and scotched body of her

husband. "Yes," she said. "That's him." He lay on his back so she could not see that the rest of his head was missing.

Her friend Nancy Clarke, though as stricken as Scarlett by the news, kept Troy for the remainder of the early morning. White and ghostlike, the moon set into a tangle of trees and clouds but in less than an hour, golden sunlight spilled into the kitchen from the east.

"Are they sure the body is Michael's?" Nancy asked. Scarlett at first did not answer. There was no answer to that.

But "Yes," she said. Nancy sat still and silent. Tears ran like miniature rivers into the corners of her mouth.

Scarlett sat later, in the silent living room, after it was over, and hugged her son. She explained to him as best she could that his father was not coming back.

"It's like he's sleeping," she explained. "But he won't wake up."

"Wake him up, mom."

"He won't ever wake up, Troy. He's in heaven in the sky."

Troy wanted to go up to heaven in a helicopter to get his father back.

"Did we want my Daddy to die?" he asked finally. "Can we get him back?"

Scarlett's shoulders slumped. She could not cry. The loss was inevitable. There was no feeling left. Numbness paralyzed her arms. "No, Troy."

Michael Kane's wife clung to their son, late into the next night, and slept with the boy and his cat in their room with the purple walls and the white goatskin rug, in the smooth double bed, with the shining floors and the immaculate dresser, the bottles on top glinting in the moonlight.

After the funeral, when their friends, her sisters, and their parents and other family had gone home, Scarlett lay alone in their bedroom, twisted with longing. She tasted bile in her throat, her gut throbbed, and she cursed her husband for dying so young and leaving her alone with a child, an aching yearning body, and an empty bed. She began to cry. Michael's cat, Rocker Patch, curled up next to her and the little boy, almost on the boy's chest, and was small comfort in reminding her of her loss.

12

Years later in Calder, Scarlett's friend Leela somber and cool sent the boys and her daughter off to school, her own children to the Catholic school across from her pretty white house, and Troy with his bag of books to the Protestant elementary school behind that.

Leela thought of the tragic past and the uncertainty of the future, shimmering in the sunshine like exhaust fumes on an early morning dewy road to *terminus*.

Her late husband Joachim always said that a man who had an affair with his secretary was not a real man, as his desire was beneath his station in life. He himself would have sex with his female supervisor if he had one, he jokingly said, and Leela believed him, the brains of his mentally vanquished colleagues giving him strength and cunning. Leela knew that Scarlett suspected her husband's secretary was the *femme fatale* at the end of the long night's journey to death seven years ago. How dreadful, she thought, to have a husband one can't trust. She smiled when she thought of her Joachim, so strong and dark, and such a loving husband and father.

When their mutual friend and neighbor Dorothy Smith

strode by on her early morning walk from the bungalow on the far side of the street, Leela found the resolve from her meditation over the second cup of tea to call to the striking auburn-haired woman.

Dorothy's arms pumped the rhythm of her hike and her fingers stroked the white ghost of a cigarette. She stopped at Leela's greeting. Leela stood on the front porch of her flower-bedecked home with the door ajar.

"Want to stop for a cup of coffee?" called Leela to her friend. "I heard the school buzzer ring a few minutes ago. We're safe."

"Why aren't you getting ready for work?" asked Dorothy, as she stopped and ground out the butt under the heel of her manly walking shoe. "The City won't like it if you're late all the time because of the kids. You must be sleeping with your boss to get all the time off that you get. Or are social workers special?"

"My supervisor Boris knows the situation." Leela closed the door behind her and stood on the steps, one lean hand cradling her cup of tea while the other stroked the wrought iron railing that ran up the side of the carpeted stairs to the rustic cedar front door. "I'm working part-time," she reminded Dorothy.

"Except for summers, when I get two months off. We're comfortable. No need to complain. And if I wanted to sleep with someone, I'd choose someone much handsomer than Boris!"

Dorothy strode up the curving front walk and sat on the bottom of the front steps. "Have one of these." She offered a crumpled pack of cigarettes to Leela, who took one and ran her hand through the short dark swing of her hair.

"I'm trying to quit. But okay, just this once." Dorothy struck a match and lit the cigarette for her friend. Leela drew hard on the cork-tipped stick before she turned around and pushed on the door behind her. Joachim had hated her smoking. Even now, six years after his death, her gut felt uneasy as she drew again on the cancer stick. She ground it out on the side of the concrete step.

A few minutes later she brought out a cup of steaming coffee with a spoon in it, and placed it in Dorothy's hand. "I hope you don't mind instant. It was too early to make a full pot."

"I like it. Speaking of early, who do you see over there coming to join us? Our mysterious neighbor."

"Intrigue, for sure," Leela agreed.

Dorothy grinned and waved exuberantly at Scarlett's tall form which cut across the street to Leela's house, where the hollyhocks ran up the California stucco walls almost to the red cedar shingles.

The three neighbors settled each on a step, and surveyed their world beyond Leela's cotoneaster hedge.

"Troy was all right last night?" asked his mother.

"Why wouldn't he be?" demanded Dorothy, and ran her fingers over her reddish crown. "It was late and they played outside until after eight. They probably fell asleep as soon as their heads hit the pillows."

Scarlett laughed, the sound like the tinkling of too many bells. "No, I don't think so. Leela?"

"Of course not, dear. They didn't settle down until almost eleven. This morning they were up at six. What a bunch."

"Did he eat?"

"Oh, yes. It took him twenty minutes to eat his toast and egg, but he did it. He sure is a wiry fellow, isn't he, Scarlett? Going to be tall like you say Michael was."

They could hear the rumble of traffic on 132nd Avenue a block away. A motorcycle coughed. At St. Edmund school across the street a buzzer blared and a few minutes later the children spilled out onto the playground at the side.

Leela waved as she saw Daisy bounding with the others to the monkey bars. She swung from the high bars, showing off for her mom and her mom's friends. Scarlett knew that Troy stood alone at the side of Calder's fence and watched the others play, because his best friend was at home sick, and he was a shy boy.

He and Stevie Cardinal often held hands and usually walked to school together, but Stevie was home sick with chickenpox, and Scarlett was worried that Troy would bring it home with him. She was uneasy with children's illnesses and had never herself had chickenpox – most of all, she was afraid of the resulting shingles if it happened later in life. Of course, she would nurse her son over it and take him to the pediatrician, but she was not born to a nurse's role and worried about death.

But the morning was fresh, clean, and bright, and the three neighbors sat and smoked and gossiped over their midmorning coffee and tea. They chatted happily for another hour until the children raced home for lunch.

Scarlett spent the rest of the day cleaning her "blue house" until it sparkled and smelled like fresh furniture polish and floor wax, so welcome in the middle of bad memories that Dorothy insisted smelled bad.

* * *

Troy's one good friend at Calder School protected him from the usual small cruelties of childhood and the proximity of a school of another faith, the students of St. Edmund and Calder being perpetually at war with one another. Today and for another week Troy bounded home alone and crouched with his cat Rocker in front of their new RCA color television, state of the art without tubes, and he prayed the Coyote would catch the Roadrunner just this once. And eat him!

Scarlett smiled.

Then night came and with it the nightmares. In her dreams, Troy rode behind his father to a crescendo of gobbling robots and music that swelled in her brain even after she awoke. She often dreamed that a small boy was cold in her arms and saved from a cold ditch of cold water. Awakening, Scarlett would realize she'd thrown off the covers and the window was open.

Ever-present in Scarlett's little house with the flat roof and the porch out back hissed the ghost of a memory. Troy's red curtains trembled, though the windows were open only an inch, and wind soughed through the corners of the room with the clown painted on the wall opposite his bed, just like at their last house. Where Scarlett had slept last night in her room, an invisible presence leaned to kiss the rumpled pillow.

Midmorning traffic rumbled by on 132nd Avenue. A motorcycle backfired. Though Rocker slept with Troy, the cat was skittish and often disappeared for long periods of time roaming through the house, crying at shadows and spooking down the hallways. The cat drove Scarlett mad at these times.

Michael's picture holding a sleeping baby leaned against a flower pot on Troy's white dresser. Michael Kane looked like President John Kennedy. In death the funeral directors, not having a picture, arranged his hair wrong and he did not look like himself. Scarlett had to tell them how to comb it.

She insisted that her husband be buried with the ruby ring she had given him for his twenty-first birthday celebration on August 15, 1963, two years before their marriage.

The funeral director, she knew now, had taken the ring because it was against the law to bury jewelry with the ... the dead. The deceased, the departed one, as the man had murmured obsequiously.

Yes, he had objected, but she hadn't listened, and now, what happened to the ring? She didn't want to think of the corpse in the simple casket, the man sheltered by the satin lining and the smooth pine of the wood. The skeleton by now, the dust left by worms.

In a later life, she would have burned the remains –

cremated her husband to a clean and final death. But that was 1971 and cremation was not a common option.

Cremation was forbidden at that time by the Catholic church, explained Leela in answer to Scarlett's question. The body must be whole to present to the Lord at the day of judgment. Scarlett thought this was a bunch of hooey. She didn't laugh because perhaps it would have hurt Leela's rather innocent allegiance to her husband's faith. Scarlett didn't want to be responsible for hurt feelings between herself and her friend.

Still, she laughed later.

She thought of Michael, so tall and lean and handsome, with the broad shoulders and the blond hair that fell like Jack Kennedy's over his forehead. With the white bell bottom jeans and the black buttons in a bulging row over his groin. She swallowed and hated him again for dying and leaving her alone.

13

Scarlett wondered if Michael's presumed mistress had been at the funeral. It was Scarlett's triumph, though, that she had been the wife behind the dark curtains, and had stood by the casket as it lowered into the hole they dug. Her family had taken pictures, and she had looked not so sad as she should have, but stunned with less than grief and more like regret at the words not said as he roared away on the Honda motorcycle to a mysterious destination or assignation.

Then in the yellow house they shared at the time of Michael's death, and here in the blue house with the leaning porch, the flat roof, and the red twigged hedge, Michael's son was joined by the real mystery of a life that might have been, an annulment of all that had actually happened, and a dream that became fact for the grieving family left behind.

The red curtains moved again, and something slipped into the boy's room through the crack of the window, or maybe through the walls that scratched like mice trying to escape a cosmic kitten.

The phone rang at midnight that night. No one answered it.

A supernatural presence slipped into their lives. Scarlett

and eventually Troy welcomed the strange father and husband. The ghost of an unremarkable past became a salvation of salvaged memories and hopes combined, the resurrection of a family torn apart by deceit, and reunited in the middle of each night and the beginning of each day, sometimes at noon or dinnertime, or bedtime for the boy, of a benevolent presence that promised redemption and an erasing of the past – who knew what harm the bright early years had delivered, and the hopelessness of a dark night rising?

In their brains scratched loving but confusing memories, as Michael intermittently seemed in retrospect more caring than she. She had to admit it. The fault though shared was hers. Now the redress was also hers.

Scarlett was eager to embrace her husband's incorporeal recall. His cat stared at empty spaces in a corner of the hallway, tracking an invisible presence and purred for no reason when the lights flickered.

How she knew it was Michael's spirit she wasn't sure, but Scarlett felt the love he had so seldom shown her overflow and spill into the recesses of the little house, and especially a young father's protectiveness toward their son.

Troy grew restive yet thoughtful as he approached his eighth birthday in April – the Legos and G.I. Joe left untouched for evenings in a row, his homework neatly spread on the kitchen table under the harsh overhead light, and his mother pencilling in her Candle Party Lite appointments for the next month on the calendar she carried with her everywhere now.

Reminders of clients and friends whom she met at these home parties helped to overcome the loneliness that plagued her at night when Troy had gone to bed and the phone was silent.

Dark corners opened up to vistas of memory as she gazed past the kitchen table to the distant years, when Michael had found her incomplete and she had found in herself an insufferable lack of love that swirled back to childhood.

She ignored any affectionate overtures he might have made to her, which were sometimes but not often offered in desperation to make up for the guilt of being an incomplete husband and father, spilling over into rage against women and children, and his mother who had nurtured the hatred.

"Mom," Troy lamented, "Did we want daddy to die?"

The walls shuddered and the windows wept. She put out her hand and touched a ghostly caress. "No." But it was a lie.

The appointment book filled up. Neat rows of names and addresses, phone numbers, and then the Rolodex to be readied as she ensured there were back-ups for each entry, and a plan for each week, usually a Friday afternoon and Saturday evening – the home parties to be planned, the insurance to be put in place in case of breakage, the suitcases full of Party Lite Candles and scents.

Her customers eagerly awaited their prizes of hints of romance and evening glamor. The neat ledger book of credits and debits for her accountant at the end of the year, the almost unused car gassed up and serviced, the nuances and details of a home business meticulously looked after – Scarlett was a businesswoman, but she felt her job was inconsequential. Her present life wasn't enough to enable her to feel mighty and in control as Nancy had reminded her before she left the old neighborhood, but she was fierce and, as her mother often said, "believed in being strong when everything seemed to be going wrong."

Scarlett smiled at nothing in the deepness of night. She would see his ghost soon enough, not just the touch of his hand on her shoulder.

14

The next afternoon, at her kitchen table while their children were at school, Scarlett confided in her best friend, Leela.

"You have no idea of a future for yourself?" Leela asked and poured milk into her Chai tea. "Is that what's wrong? What about Troy? You have to be strong for him."

The kitchen curtains swayed as though in a breeze, but the day was still.

Leela continued, "It's the angst of our times. There's a softball practice going on after the men come home from work. 'For married people,' I'm told. No wonder we have no goals. We're nothing alone. Goals are for complete women. They tell us we're not complete.

"What's the point of it, anyhow? My in-laws in India keep asking me when I'm coming home again to find another man. I think they have one picked out for me."

"I'm not nothing. Neither are you."

Leela jiggled the spoon in her cup. "There's a spirit in us that connects when our men are gone. That comes alive. You've felt it."

"Yes."

"When the husbands go off to war, or to work, or to hunt – the women's spirits grow to take the place that has been usurped by the men while they were here. It's not that we're incomplete *without* them. We're incomplete when they're *here*."

"I think so." Uneasy and wanting to change the subject, Scarlett checked her watch. "The kids should be home from school soon."

"Yes, and what then?" Leela's breath was like a gust of dismay. "What about my Daisy? Will she grow up to be like us?"

"Of course. The boys will grow up to be like their fathers."

Her friend sipped on the hot sweet liquid. "There's change in the air."

She had not successfully altered the course of Leela's conversation, deeper than Scarlett appreciated. "The times they are a-changin'," agreed Scarlett. "But too slow for us."

"I don't think so. I'm thinking of joining the women's movement."

"You? Would your culture forbid it? Besides, what do we need with a movement? We have ourselves, pal. And I have memories of what I could have done differently, if I hadn't been trapped in the box of my upbringing, the anger, the lack of love, the indifference to a marriage that was expected of me. I've determined I'm going to fight for myself and use the anger I feel to make a better life for myself and my son."

"*Why'd* you get married, Scarlett?" Leela leaned forward.

Outside, the buzzer sounded to alert them that Oliver School, Troy's class, had let out for the day. A few minutes later, a more muted buzzer signalled the students would be home soon from St. Edmund School. Scarlett frowned.

"My mother raised me to expect it, I guess. I never thought of anything else; a career, maybe, university maybe, but lack of funds and lack of ambition kept me from it - or ambition misplaced, into a husband rather than a career.

"A high school guidance counselor discouraged me from joining the military as I wanted, because the service women were 'not feminine and not good role models.' I wanted to be a pilot. Women aren't allowed to be pilots in the RCAF; did you know that? I would have been a clerk."

Leela frowned. "I didn't know that. I didn't know you wanted to be in the Air Force. Wasn't your brother in the Air Force?"

"No, both my brothers stayed on the farm. My mother is very proud of them and my three sisters, who married well. Me? I'm Michael's wife.

"I know nothing of his family. He was estranged from them at an early age. They're a mystery to me. Just like I'm a mystery to my own family. I have two brothers and three sisters. All gone from me in spirit many years ago, the brothers on the family farm and my sisters married young and with families of their own, far away. Only two came to Michael's funeral."

"Like many women married to forceful men and from a traditional family who stressed obedience at all costs, you'd think that you're a non-entity on your own. I was the same," said Leela.

Scarlett got up to place cookies on a plate for Troy for later when he came rushing in. She opened the heavy door of the Kenmore Harvest Gold refrigerator and found the pitcher of orange Tang.

"I'm not a non-entity, Leela. Not any more. With Michael gone and my parents in their own puddle no longer demanding I be an obedient good child, I'm striking out."

She continued, "I think there's a slanting of sunshine through the forest to illuminate the truth, like those religious posters I've seen. He speaks to me at night, did you know that?"

"Who? Michael?"

"Yes. Troy hears him, too. He wants me to be wonderful," Scarlett said. "He wants me to be happy."

Leela shrugged. "Maybe he always did."

"He hit me once." Scarlett's voice was flat. "We were going to a marriage counselor together, who said it was my fault."

"Your fault he hit you?"

"Yes. That's what the marriage counselor said."

"Was it a male marriage counselor?"

"Of course."

"How can you forgive him?" Leela asked and poured more tea.

"Who?"

"The counselor, of course."

"Not Michael?"

"Michael, too."

"He drank and fooled around," Scarlett admitted.

"There's no forgiving; there's just bad times and good times. The good times had to make way for the bad. It's possible to still love a piece of shit."

"That's how it is."

"What does the ghost say?"

Scarlett crossed the shining linoleum and sat again across from her friend. "Do you believe it's a ghost? That he does not rest in peace?"

"In India we have a belief, after the departed has been burned on the pyre, we say that their soul does not have such a long and endless wait after death, where Christians would say, 'rest in peace', till you are finally raised again for judgment and eternal happiness or suffering thereafter.

"In Dharmic philosophies the dead immediately gets reborn and based on his karma (the good and bad deeds in past lives), either moves on to planes higher and more pleasurable than the one which he departed from, or to states more severe and painful. Dharmic philosophies also claim that these more pleasurable or more painful states are as temporary as the life the deceased passed over from and thus not eternal."

Scarlett chewed on her bottom lip and frowned. "I don't think that allows for ghosts."

"Maybe he's stuck between states."

"I'm not a Hindu nor am I a Christian," Scarlett declared. "But I feel my husband in these rooms, Leela, and he is here to make amends, I'm sure. He loved us."

"It doesn't sound like it."

"It was his way."

Leela frowned. "Then he is not reborn immediately? His karma is so inconclusive? If you look into the science of it, my friend, you'll find reincarnation is more than a possibility."

"I don't believe in being born again or past lives, though science might support it, as you say." Scarlett turned around and found that Troy was watching her with wide trusting eyes.

15

"I'm hungry, mom." The young boy kissed his mother and grabbed two cookies from the plate in one dirty fist.

"Wash your hands first, young man," Scarlett ordered.

Cramming the cookies into his mouth, Troy mumbled on his way down the hallway, "Hello, Mrs. Balakrishnan."

"Hello, Troy." Leela laughed and began to clear the cups from the table. "It's time to go," she said. "My children will be home and Daisy can't control my willful son."

"I hope you're right about Michael," commented Scarlett. "I hope he has a better life ahead of him after death."

"I didn't say that exactly," Leela said and hugged her friend goodbye. "But if it makes you feel better about it, then I hope so, too.

"You must remember that I'm Hindu first, though my husband was a Catholic and I promised to raise our family as Catholics. Still, as a woman from India, my beliefs are colored by the culture that surrounded us and my family's faith. I don't pray to your Christian God."

"Neither do I," Scarlett admitted.

That night the closet door creaked open and a wedge of

moonlight illuminated the space within. Scarlett got up out of the bed she had bought for herself when she and Troy moved into the "blue house," and checked inside the closet just to make sure there were no monsters hiding in there. She checked under her bed.

Smiling at her foolishness, she closed the closet door and got back into bed. She pulled the striped cotton sheet up over her chin and fluffed the down pillow under her head. The closet door creaked open again.

She closed her eyelids tightly, and began uncharacteristically to pray. She'd almost forgotten how, remembered only vaguely from her mother's teachings as a girl, but began a childish prayer that ended, "If I die before I wake...*I pray the Lord my soul to take...gentle Jesus meek and mild, pity me, a little child...*"

The lace curtains at the window moved, although there was no wind. From the depths of the dark outside, a memory stirred. Scarlett huddled closer beneath the satin quilt and the striped sheet, and felt comfort in knowing that the presence was more benign in death than in life.

16

Troy called out from the next room, "Mom?" but was met with silence. A light shone on the walls of his bedroom and he lay, petrified, with Rocker Patch purring at his feet, until Scarlett responded and opened the door, finding only darkness, a cat, and a frightened little boy.

She took them with her into the soft double bed in her own room, and they nestled together while a noiseless wind ruffled the curtains. She kept the bedside light on to keep at bay the fear.

A deep comfortable voice hummed, "Ballad of Easy Rider" until morning, but that might have been a dream. They both heard it, though. The voiceless almost noiseless music didn't frighten Troy, but seemed to give him comfort. The orange cat purred at their feet.

"Orange tabbies all came from Vikings," Michael had explained, on bringing home the small dust bunny of a kitten. "Marmalades have great temperaments."

Scarlett reached out her hand in the direction of the dawn and grasped the pale fingers of her dead husband. "You've come to rescue us, haven't you?" she murmured, and he didn't answer directly, but hummed some more.

The light in her bedroom flickered out as the sun rose, as though someone forced the switch. Scarlett felt that the kind entity was simply another side of Michael's confused spirit, as he was in life, but it was hard to reconcile the presence of good with the malevolence she felt when Michael's overarching wings had enveloped them both in life.

Seldom had her husband admitted to a fond heart, though he cried out for love and understanding. He was a simple man. She more complicated than he, was unable to comprehend his basic nature. They should never have met and, having met, should never have married. Her heart palpitated.

A plan crystalized in Scarlett's imagination. A bolt of power raced up the chakras in her spine. Michael's old hobby work tools, the appliance parts, gears, miniature gasoline drums, rivets, and small motors remained in a locked storage room in the basement of her newly purchased house in Calder. She had carried them in six wooden boxes from their rented yellow house, unable to let go of this last vestige of her life with him.

Now she determined she would construct a remedy to the spell, a beating soul in the midst of her memories so that Troy would grow tall and strong, and without the legacy possessed from the grave of his caring father; his grievous father – one who lived again as he should not in the souls of the aware.

The fire in her brain ignited, and though her memories were overwhelming, her resolve was even greater.

17

Scarlett remembered the circus Michael had taken them to for Troy's third birthday, one of the good times until the end, when the ringmaster screamed the praises of his pretty circus women, the lions roared, the clown waved at their son, and her husband cried.

The year was 1971 and April 17 was the first Saturday after Easter, when a small local fair played at the Beverley Bandstand not far from their home. Troy remembered it, too; the day his father sat with head in his broad tough hands and tears squeezed with great hulking gulps from between his fingers.

Their excursion started well. Getting to the Bandstand early, Michael parked their white Chevette, which had taken the place of the Sprite when Troy was born, on a graveled site in a nearby residential area and they walked a couple of blocks to the bleachers.

Overhead dipped, swayed, and huffed bright hot air balloons touching so close to the bandstand they could see the pale faces of the passengers leaning over the baskets. White cirrus clouds chased the tail of winds and Mister Sol burned

golden like butter above the little boy and his parents on this
happy occasion.

Worn smooth by countless bottoms, the wooden benches
stretched from where they sat in the second from the front row
to the bleachers high above. "We got good seats," commented
Michael as they sat, his arm around Scarlett. He hugged her
and the boy closer. "It was worth it to leave early."

There was only one ring in the circus and the elephants
were small. The velvet smooth and orange striped big cats
snarled, a few in their cages while the brightly costumed big cat
trainer wrapped an arm around the neck of the nearest tiger
and nuzzled the big cat's ear. A line of chorus girls leaped and
threw their pom poms into the air.

A clown popped up over the fence and Troy gasped with
delight. Clowns had not yet earned a bad reputation. Small
dogs jumped through hoops. A clever cat soared through three
blazing circlets and the trainer rewarded it with treats as it
pranced back to the podium and calculated the distance once
again. The trainer moved the far chair closer. The cat leaped.

Troy held his breath then applauded wildly. "Just like
Rocker Patch!" the boy called. His pudgy little hands were red
with clapping.

"Yes, hun," Michael replied, adjusting a cup of coffee and
the large bag of pink popcorn in one hand while holding the
boy and his mother with the other arm. "See the ponies?"

There were indeed spotted ponies which pranced on dainty
hoofs while pretty girls dressed in purple and white tutus
balanced bravely on their backs. Music soared. The crowd
clapped and cheered.

A lion, King of Beasts, roared as the ringmaster cracked a
whip for effect and nothing else, and announced the acts one
by one. Far overhead, a man walked a high wire and the
Bolshoi Family swung from a flying trapeze.

"Wow, mom! Look at that! The man is flying!" Troy dipped a

grubby hand into the bag of popcorn and stuffed the pink kernels into his "O" of a mouth. Popcorn scattered down his little jacket and stuck to his pants. "Watch out, daddy, he fall on us."

Michael's handsome face beamed at his son. "His friend is going to catch him. See? They've done this hundreds of times before."

Scarlett snuggled into her husband's rare embrace and spoke to Troy. "Dear, do you have to go to the bathroom? Mommy can take you. Do you want a drink?"

"Pop, please, mom?"

"Okay. This time we'll get you a pop." She motioned to the hawker who strode down the stairs to their row. "Two orange pops, please."

Michael waved a ten-dollar bill. "We'll have three hotdogs, too, please, boy. Hold the mustard on one."

"Yes, sir." The fresh-faced young man reached into his bag of goodies and arranged the snacks in a cardboard box with cut-outs for the soda pop. "Here you are, sir. Thanks a lot, that's great!" As Michael added a dollar for a tip.

"Have to pee-pee, mom." Troy bounced up and down on the worn wooden seat. "Right now!"

"Okay, dear," Scarlett said and Michael objected, "No, darling, I'll take him."

The man and his son made their way past the first two rows of seats while Scarlett sipped on a drink. The circus performers paraded in the ring in front of her.

She reflected on their good fortune, to be sitting here this day, with their child and the bright breeze, the balloons, and the circus spread out in front of them, and the love between them.

She settled contentedly in her seat. She caught a glimpse of the tall blond man with the western shirt, the tight jeans, and the large belt buckle making his way back to sit beside her, and the small boy trustingly holding his hand. Her heart swelled with emotion.

As they made themselves comfortable beside her again, she thought, *this can't last*, and she did the unthinkable. Again.

"You know our marriage is on the rocks," she said to no one in particular, whispering really, so that Troy would not hear. Michael jerked his hand away from her shoulders.

One bright glance from icy blue eyes, a crestfallen face, the forgotten coffee cold beside him, and the day ruined.

She had done it and didn't think a thing of it until much later, now in Leela's house after her husband and her son and the day was long over, five years ago and in another world, another time, and another life she had managed to destroy with the man she had vowed to love until death did them part. She had after all stayed with him until death. And beyond, it seemed.

But the death of their marriage far preceded his horrific accident, suicide or not, and the desperate rush of the big Honda down a rain slick road to an assignation with a mistress or not, and the ambulance attendants picking up the remains of the red bloodied body on the red bloodied street below the precipitous bridge.

"Our marriage?" His eyes were cast down. Troy looked up, innocently.

"On the rocks. For a long time now."

Scarlett had no excuse that day at the circus. She wasn't drinking alcohol at that time. The drinking came later. With the guilt.

"I love you, Scarlett."

She didn't answer. Later she was able to understand what she had done, and who she had done it to, and why it was not an unforgiveable sin, but rather someone who loved her very much forgave her and the anger in her veins.

18

Years later, a mental illness like a paranoid psychosis struck her. It started in the bottom of her stomach like an iron rod, twisted, and stayed there. The Freudian marriage therapist Lawrence Tumulak didn't foresee it. It had started with the post-partum depression after the birth of Troy and the therapist had not addressed it.

Lawrence blamed her for the sad marriage. She blamed herself but blamed Michael most of all. She lived with anger. *The Circus years ago, when Troy was barely three, and his father would die in two months.*

"Daddy?"

"We'll stay until the end, son. Here come the elephants. Look at them and do you hear? The circus is almost over. Wasn't it fun? Troy, always remember, though, wild animals belong in their homes in the jungle. They don't belong in a circus."

"Why they here, daddy?"

"People like to go to a circus and see wild animals. It's fun, Troy, and you can learn about creatures you don't otherwise see. It's like the zoo. Remember Storyland Valley Zoo with the seals and the monkeys?"

Scarlett fidgeted. "Sometimes zoos and circuses rescue animals that otherwise might die," she commented. Michael nodded. Troy beamed at his mom and dad and they all held hands and left with the other audience members, filing out of the stands with happy faces.

"Daddy cry, Mom?"

Scarlett frowned. "Mommy said something sad and it wasn't true, dear. Don't think about it again."

"Your fault, mom?"

Michael swung him by the arms around in the parking lot and Troy screamed with delight. Scarlett smiled, but the harm had been done.

Troy always remembered that his father had taken him to a circus when he was three, and that his father cried at the circus, and he didn't understand why. He was only a little boy, after all, and his father was only a little boy, too. Really – in his head.

His bloodied and fractured head. The engines he made in his workshop marched on past his mortality and haunted Scarlett's dreams until she finished them, in her blue house with the green hedge and the drunken fence.

Men thought that Scarlett was beautiful in appearance and form, and didn't realize she kept herself beautiful because she was so ugly inside.

* * *

The mental illness spread and snaked inside her in the old place after Michael died, but it was short-lived and an addiction which died, too, when she stopped drinking, moved to Calder, and met John and her other new neighbors. The geographical cure, and it worked!

It was a sort of obsessive disorder, a splitting of her psyche into the good mom and the bad mom. The drinking was all she could do for a couple of years until, without a therapist, she took herself to a Twelve Step program. There is no cure but Scarlett stopped.

Her new friends in AA thought a higher power cured her. No, the illness burned itself out, the guilt that caused it and the anger burned out like a long explosive smoldering cord that when it reached the keg of TNT finally just fizzled.

She threw a big bucket of water on it. That's all. She told herself that she wasn't to blame for her husband's anger. Scarlett, never innocent nor pure, met her husband's devastated ghost at the end and healed it. She confronted her own anger, drank it to death, and survived. An awful long cold winter of years and tears led to the cure.

For Scarlett and Michael, their human condition sprang from an inheritance of vipers, a mass of snakes that dropped from the dust of love then indifference – first to hatred and finally back to love as the seasons rolled on.

She was strong but not in the ways most people think. If she fell, she rose up even stronger because she was a survivor and not a victim. Never completely in control, all the struggling women in her world were invincible at the end. Like Audrey Hepburn, they believed that happy girls are pretty girls and they believed in miracles. A miracle was about to happen.

19

"Hand me the screwdriver, Troy," his mother murmured as she held out an open palm. The ten-year-old boy shivered but complied.

Her crystals lay in a pile beside her on the worktable. An astrological chart she'd been working on was crumpled in one corner. In the next two minutes the temperature in the workshop dropped by yet another five degrees Celsius, heralding the presence of lost souls.

Scarlett wiped her nose with the sleeve of her wool sweater. "Thank you, son." Steam hissed from the three-quarter inch black steel pipes in front of her. Gears clattered.

Into the bubbling liquid in the Erlenmeyer flask she dropped a tincture of *Hypericum perforatum*. Although barely three o'clock in the afternoon Mountain Standard time, the high dirty window in the workshop flickered with overtones of sleet heralding an approaching storm.

Troy pursed his lips and leaned closer. She pushed him back to a more secure distance. "There's a blizzard coming, mom." The overhead fluorescent lamps hummed and their white glare blinked as a sudden gale pelted the little house.

"We're safe in here, hun," she said. "Don't worry. Your father's tools have rubber handles and a good strong grip. Nothing can hurt us unless it's that damn phone."

"Did you get another wrong number, mommy?"

"No, Troy. It was nothing." The bulbs in the low ceiling sizzled.

"Was it for dad again?"

"No, Troy. We don't know who is calling, you know. Someday maybe a telephone will be smart enough to let us know who it is."

"Does the operator know?"

"I asked the telephone company to trace the call, but they don't stay on the line long enough to trace it."

"That's too bad, mom. Are they going to hurt us?"

"They haven't yet and it's been six or seven years since they started." Scarlett turned off the Bunsen burner and moved the flask with tongs to a lead plate on the other side of the iron pipes and the little steam engines.

She removed the goggles from her face.

Rocker Patch watched from across the room, curled up in an orange fluffy ball, little black dot on his pink nose. He purred, tracking an invisible presence across the opposite wall.

Troy giggled. "Now I can see you when you take the goggles off."

"Indeed, you can."

Her son leaned closer. The window turned frosty and clattered, pelted by sheets of sleet. Water dribbled down the side of the basement wall and collected in a can Scarlett had placed on the olefin carpet for just that purpose.

They could see the cotoneaster hedge at the side of the house sway, drip, and whiten with snow, but the blizzard was passing.

The tincture of St. John's Wort had bubbled and dissolved

in the Erlenmeyer flask. The gears ground grittily in the little steam engines and on the three-quarter inch iron pipes.

On the other side of the room Scarlett's ghetto blaster belched and broke the tape in the middle of a song by Jimi Hendrix. *Three more heroes dead*, she thought, although she wouldn't miss "The Ballad of Easy Rider". Maybe the broken tape was an omen of peace.

Steam popped from the wheels that turned around and around beneath the little steam engines on the table.

She wanted a cigarette. Her hand moved spasmodically and knocked the bottle of *Hypericum perforatum*, or St. John's Wort as it was more commonly called, onto the carpet. It rolled without breaking open and Troy leaned down and retrieved it by his foot. Scarlett took it from his newly washed hands.

She swirled the mixture in the flask. The aroma of turpentine-balsam spiraled into the corners of her workshop, though she would always think of it as Michael's workshop, filled as it was with his tools and equipment.

And his spirit.

"Look, mom, the sun's shining!" Her son found a leather laced football on a shelf back of the table at which Scarlett worked and began to toss it into the air and catch it. He dropped it once and kicked it to the corner of the room where – his father stood.

Smiling. Michael Kane was smiling. Scarlett had never liked it when her husband smiled. It boded something very bad for her and the boy.

Was that the wind or the aftermath of the brief storm that sighed and soughed from the corner underneath the window?

The ice-covered cotoneasters outside waved at the man in the corner of the room. He couldn't see the hedge anyway. Their red berries gleamed with snow.

Glass on a photograph on the wall opposite the table in the

basement workshop reflected splinters of light and yes, the sun was shining through the clouds.

"Get back, Troy," warned his mother, extending her right arm straight against the boy's chest. He took a backward step.

"Gosh, mom, I was just playing."

"Go upstairs, Troy. I'll be there shortly. Turn on the television and watch the cartoons for a few minutes until I get there. There's orange drink in the fridge and help yourself to cookies."

"Why, mom?

"Don't ask questions. Just go. Now."

"Oh, okay. I'm thirsty anyhow. And I don't like that awful smell," Troy said. He walked right past his father standing in the corner as though he hadn't seen him. *He doesn't see him,* thought Scarlett. *Good.*

Rocker Patch purred and rubbed against an invisible ankle.

The large bulb on top of the iron pipes flickered as a steam engine began to sputter.

"It's working," Michael breathed and padded to the center of the room, where he leaned on the table and placed his hand on the Erlenmeyer flask. *"I can smell it. I can feel it. It's getting into my bones."* Then he laughed. Scarlett shivered.

"Just don't speak the spell."

She could see him solidly against the whitewashed walls of the little basement room. Tall, handsome, blond, his mouth twisted in that familiar grin that meant trouble for her.

He wore his white bell bottom jeans buttoned with black metal disks and a dark green poet's shirt open at the collar, exposing his hairless chest. The last clothes she'd seen him in, but without the leather jacket that he wore when the Honda CB-750 crashed into the light standard at one hundred and forty kilometers per hour. The jacket that was torn and red and wet when she'd had to identify his broken body that morning in 1971.

"How did you know it was me?" he asked, as though he read

her thoughts. No longer a whisper in her brain, his voice snicked across the table at her.

"Only the back of your head was gone. Your arms and legs broken, but your face was intact. A blessing, they said."

"So, you saw my face." His eyes burned blue into hers. No wonder Troy had eyes the color of violets and that mop of blond curly hair. Two parents with such azure eyes and his father with such tawny locks. "I wasn't such a mess, then."

"You were. They'd cleaned you up somewhat but your legs and arms..."

Michael barked like a dog. "They were twisted? Broken? Gone altogether?"

She hung her head. "I don't know. I can't remember."

"Sure, you can. Try to remember," he urged.

"I can't, Michael. I don't want to. You must go now. You *will* go. I demand it."

He folded his arms. "Darling, you can't make demands of me."

Scarlett rose from her chair, her eyes like ovals of blue ice. She swept the clattering pipes and engines to one side. The steam screamed and the bulb flashed translucent with bright yellow bars inside, glowing, bright, brighter – she flicked a small iron switch on the side of the pipes and the gears clattered and roared, the engines rocked and bellowed and the propellers whirled.

The flask of *Hypericum perforatum* bubbled again where she had placed it on top of the steam in a special container, and the Pyrex glass began to shake. She added a few drops of a chemical to the liquid hell and it began to boil and spat crimson and mellow yellow pineapple fire.

"I've always loved you," Michael's image whispered.

He cowered in the corner, moving back several steps with sandaled feet. The metal and plastic gears chattered. The contraption Scarlett had created spread the length of the table and towered from the tabletop thigh-high to her five feet eight-inch frame. The fluorescent lamps that hung from the low ceiling swung and flashed.

"I love you now," he said in a firmer voice and put out a pale hand covered with fine golden fuzz.

She longed to feel the warmth of his hand, but feared in the coldness of the little room that he had brought the freeze with him, and that his hand would be solid and icy like his voice had been.

He whistled the song from "Wild Mountain Thyme" and she covered her ears. "I don't want to hear that, Michael. It was suicide, wasn't it?"

"Was it?" He grinned. "Why would I do that to you and my darling son? He was only three. You were twenty-six. See, you think I don't remember, don't you? He must be – let me think. Ten now. In school for sure. How's he doing?"

"Do you care?"

"Of course, I care. The apple didn't fall far from the tree. He looks like me, doesn't he?"

"Always did," she answered.

He moved closer, the golden hair on the back of his hand soft and warm as she placed her hand over his. "Does that make it hard for you?" he asked. "That he looks like me?"

"No." He put his arms around her, awkward as always, and his touch was rough as always.

Scarlett would not cry but she refused to kiss him. He had been dead for seven years in June and she hated him.

She missed him.

She loved him.

20

Scarlett moved to the front of the table to embrace her husband. The table shook with the force of the steam engines and the propellers trying to raise the machinery from the table. Without taking her head from Michael's shoulder, she reached behind her with her left hand and turned off the contraption, which continued to quiver and spit for a couple more minutes.

Rocker Patch hissed at her and ran through the door and upstairs. She glanced out the window and thought she saw a figure run in the snow behind the corner of a building. No, it was an illusion.

Scarlett felt the roughness of Michael's whiskers on her cheek. She stroked his dear handsome face. "How did you get in here?" she asked.

"Through the door," he murmured, smiling, and she believed him because she did not think he was a ghost. He was too solid. Too real. It would have been unthinkable for him to be merely a spirit that would twist from her embrace and disappear again for another seven years. His smile seemed sincere. She relaxed.

"Mom?" Startled, they both broke apart from the awkward hug. Troy was standing in the doorway, door ajar, cookie crumbs on his face and a glass of milk in his hand. "I couldn't find any juice," he explained, holding up the milk.

"You have a white mustache, son," said Michael. He reached out to touch the boy but Troy recoiled.

"Who is this?" he asked.

"Who do you think I am?" queried Michael. Scarlett moved to their son's side and wrapped a protective arm around his slim shoulders.

"He doesn't know," she said.

"Hasn't he seen pictures?"

Scarlett shrugged. "That's not enough."

Troy slammed the glass of milk onto the table, spilling most of it. He threw the rest of the cookie onto the floor. "I don't know you! You go away now and leave my mother alone or I'm calling the cops."

His mother stood with arms empty. Her deceased husband and angry son faced one another across the room. Sunlight washed their faces in the early evening light. The fluorescent bulb hummed and flickered, and a smell of turpentine-balsam swirled from the laboratory flask.

"I can't stand that smell," Michael said. He retched.

Troy ran from the room. The door swung shut behind him.

His father shrugged and fixated Scarlett with a cerulean gaze. "I think I should go."

"Yes," she answered. "It might be wise."

He waited for her to leave the room. She hurried to their son upstairs. As she mounted the steps with her hands on the rails, she wondered if the ghost had simply vanished, or if he would leave the house like a normal person.

He certainly seemed solid enough.

21

"Coffee?" Leela asked, pouring cups all around to the four other women. "It's not instant this time. We all want to know what's kept you so busy, Scarlett. We've hardly seen you for a month. Christmas came and went and you kept to yourself."

"John's been gone these past two months and it's been harder to cope," Scarlett said. "I'm glad he's back. I guess I've come to depend on him and my friends here. Not so independent as I thought. John did come over for Christmas dinner. It was fun but no, I haven't been around, Leela. A lot of Candle Party Lite showers in the afternoons. Working on crafts in the basement and making sure Troy gets lots of sleep..." Her voice trailed off. Her movements were short and jerky. She blinked rapidly. Leela's spacious kitchen seemed claustrophobic. She wished she were home with Michael but was anxious with lack of sleep and the shock of the supernatural visions and memories best buried with him. Her neighbors exchanged glances.

Dorothy put out her cigarette in the small pewter ashtray. "What about mom? Does she get enough sleep?"

Scarlett glanced quickly at Dorothy then looked away at the clock on the kitchen wall. "Sure thing," she lied. "I do."

Penny Cardinal and Karin Sivertsen sipped at their milky coffees. Neither smoked. Leela Balakrishnan as the hostess passed a plate of oatmeal cookies around the table.

Penny cleared her throat. "My four girls and, of course, Stevie, miss playing with Troy after school. He must be busy with homework now that he's going into Grade Five next fall."

"He's a big boy now – ten years old!" Karin exclaimed. "They're all growing up so fast. I can't believe it's been four years since you first moved into our neighborhood, Scarlett. The twins aren't in his class at school this year, but he's out there at recess and on his way home to lunch, Penny. Just last Sunday I saw James and you take the family to church at ten, and Troy was with you. I thought, good for you, Scarlett and Penny! I think James would be a good influence on a young boy, being a church-going father and all that."

"It was Leela who suggested it," Scarlett commented. The normal gossiping amongst her neighbors calmed her nerves, which were tinderstruck and raw. She sucked on a cigarette and patted Leela's hand.

Penny smiled. "Foursquare Gospel has an impromptu softball game before the children's Sunday School almost every week in the spring. Troy's welcome to join in when they start up."

"It's taken us almost three years to get him to go to church with you," Scarlett replied. "Even though he seemed eager at first. I suppose if I went myself..."

"That would be ideal," Leela interrupted. "You can't expect children to enjoy church if the parents don't go."

Scarlett frowned. "I'm trying to quit smoking," she perseverated, butted the cigarette, and took another cookie. "I'm going to get fat, I'm afraid."

"You? Never!" rasped Dorothy in her alto voice and coughed. "You're thin as a stick of Juicy Fruit gum."

"My doctor gave me a prescription for nicotine gum. It helps but only if I don't smoke, of course."

"Victor tried to quit and smoked at the same time as he chewed the gum," said Karin, laughing. She nudged Dorothy, who sat next to her at the pretty table. "It's your turn to quit, Dot."

"Never!" Dorothy repeated and coughed again. She lit another Pall Mall off the glowing ember of the first before she stubbed it out.

Relieved the subject was allowed to be changed so abruptly, Scarlett felt a deep affection for her friends, who were concerned for her and Troy. She didn't admit it to anyone, but she was concerned as well and her nerves were raw as fresh hamburger.

"I should get going home," she said to her friends after the coffee cups were empty and the gossip felt empty, too, and the affairs of the day.

"Hugs," said Leela and the rest of her friends smiled and waved. "See you later. I think I hear the school buzzer now anyhow. Skating later before the ice melts?"

"Sure." They sometimes took the children to the little skating rink near John's convenience store and they all rented skates. It was a good time even though none of them were expert, and sometimes the community league rep played Skater's Waltz and other tunes over the speakers from his office in the shed. They'd flooded the rink just last week again, and if the Junior League wasn't playing hockey it would be open to the public, depending on the weather.

Scarlett looked forward to the outing as something normal that every family did in the area with children. Not seeing ghosts like she and Troy.

22

Scarlett felt watchful eyes following her as she entered the house she shared with her son. He still complained of a light in his room and scratching at the walls. *Mice,* she explained to the growing boy with the light mop of hair and searching eyes.

"It doesn't sound like mice, mom." He no longer accepted her circumferential explanations. On occasion, he saw the man who was Michael Kane standing somberly in the doorway of the workshop or in the hallway outside his room.

"I saw that man again. Who is he?"

"He's a friend, Troy. Don't let it bother you. He's like a spirit in the house. He won't hurt us."

Leela had bought him a St. Christopher's medal and a St. Nicholas medal to hang on a cord around his neck to protect him from evil spirits. Troy fondled the icons around his neck. "Would it help if we prayed, mom?"

Her neighbor, Leela, knew that something very odd was happening in the little blue house across the street from her place. Scarlett had told her, and often at midnight she saw the light in the kitchen where Scarlett sat writing invoices and paperwork for the Candle Party Lite business she still took on. At other times a light flickered in the basement where her workshop was.

Troy had been asking his mother for a baseball glove and ball for his birthday coming up in April. They were in a package on a shelf in the basement already, waiting for his birthday.

Little clockwork machines issued from that workshop, little automatons that amused the children and Scarlett's friends, but to her eyes were of no use to anyone. They marched on a track to the corner and back, and their gears whirled in unison to an ethereal music box embedded in their backs.

"All very strange," commented Leela to her eldest girl, Daisy. Leela was the most superstitious of the group of friends, and she crossed herself when she saw Scarlett's hunched figure sitting night by night behind the thin curtains of the house across the street.

There was a man, too, seldom seen and never spoken of, and it wasn't John Aguila from the convenience store who had taken a shine to Scarlett right away. John delivered loaves of bread and bottles of milk every Monday afternoon or evening, He would trudge back to his rooms behind the store quite crest-fallen after those trips, Scarlett waving goodbye from the porch. Leela was happy that she noticed John was sometimes invited in, especially for the holidays which he seemed to have split between his mother's place and Scarlett's hospitality.

Leela was observant and caring, and perhaps, thought her good friends, a little too engaged in Scarlett's business. But they were all worried about their friend. She grew thinner and paler, and dark circles appeared beneath her eyes.

Bidding goodbye to her friends, Scarlett scurried across the street to her house a few minutes before the Calder school bell rang for dismissal. Troy was tearing across the schoolyard now, coat flying behind him. A chorus of "See ya tomorrow" followed him. Stevie Cardinal stood looking after him. "See ya, Stevie!" he called.

She thought of the visits to their house she no longer welcomed from friends of hers and her son's. Almost weeping, Scarlett stood at the door as Michael enveloped her into his arms. Troy gave him scarcely a glance as he rushed past into the kitchen, so used was he to the apparition, and so thoughtless of its meaning and its connection to the sounds and visions in their home.

Outside, John Aguila had left a bottle of milk, a loaf of bread, and a bag of candy. "Damn," she said again, "I wish he wouldn't bother anymore. Now I owe him five dollars. The Christmas dinner with him seems to have held me ransom. Damn."

"He wants you to come see him at the store, mom," Troy chortled, plucking an apple from a bowl in the kitchen. "Can I have a glass of juice, please?"

Michael's arms seemed solid. The expression on his face was sullen. He made a slight growling noise in his throat. Scarlett slipped out of his grasp. Troy watched with wide eyes.

"Oh-oh," he said. "The man's mad."

"Don't say that, dear," cautioned Scarlett.

Michael beamed at his son. "Right you are, son," he said. "We don't want another man coming around here, do we? The two of us are good enough for mom, aren't we?"

Troy regarded him. "I guess. Would you like to see my new robot?"

"Why not? When you're fifteen I'll get you a motorbike and teach you how to tinker with it."

"Mrs. Balakrishnan says the apple doesn't fall far from the tree," Troy offered. He munched on the fruit and spilled some juice. Scarlett flushed as she wiped up the mess.

"Over my cold and dead body, you will," she said to Michael.

Michael ran cold dead hands along her bare arms. "That can be arranged." He snickered.

She put her hands in her pockets and clenched her jaw. She controlled her nerves through sheer force of will.

Michael turned and like a normal person, walked out the front door. An engine coughed on the street and screamed northeast like a wild thing on the icy streets. "That's him," Troy said. "Why does he come around, anyhow?"

Scarlett pressed her hands and nose to the window. Leela was watching from across the street.

"What's for supper?" Troy asked. "I hope it isn't fish. I don't like fish."

Scarlett shrugged. "Last week you liked fish."

"Last week I didn't like that strange man much, either, mom. Why do you let him in the house? He's creepy. Not when he's nice like today. But he can be mean to you. My robots don't like him, either. They march right away from him when I set them up. Creepy."

"Don't talk like that about your father, dear." His mother sighed and took her hands out of her pockets. She could feel a burning in her stomach.

"He's not my father. My father is dead." Troy threw his book bag across the kitchen and stomped down the hall to his room. Scarlett shook her head.

"We'll fight it, you and me," she said.

"We want him dead!" Troy blubbered, and his door slammed.

23

There was silence in the little house, then the mice began – *scritch scritch scritch* – behind the walls – the lights flickered, and a long piece of wallpaper peeled off, exposing dead drywall and a weeping trickle of moisture that ran down the ivy pattern onto the white baseboard.

Murky liquid pooled like tears on the white and red linoleum squares beneath Scarlett's feet, "I'm not defeated," she declared. "We have only begun to fight.

"The love we missed out on all those years, Troy," she called down the hallway to his room, "The love that should have been ours, son – we will have that!"

"You're crazy!" Troy cried. She could hear his automatons march and crash against the door to his room.

She checked her watch, with the square face and the three dials to measure time across the globe. Eight o'clock. Troy was tired and she should put him to bed. She was tired, too.

The dial phone hanging on the kitchen wall pealed and rang and trilled, and Scarlett didn't answer it, but sat with a thud on a chrome chair under the window.

Is Michael Kane there?

Scarlett remembered the old stories and the recent tales of horror and hauntings right here in Edmonton.

La Boheme Restaurant, a romantic spot where she had often longed to visit for bed and breakfast, looked beautiful on the outside but what happened inside was not. Rumors told a tale of a caretaker of the building savagely murdering his wife and chopping her body into little pieces. He left the pieces in the boiler room. Guests said they could hear the sound of a body being dragged down the stairs.

A theatre was rumored to be haunted by a jilted bride who had hanged herself upstairs in the 1920s. She would appear in the lobby by the staircase or in the projection room.

The ghosts would not leave, just as Michael would never leave her. Did she want him to leave them alone?

No. She decided no. She wanted her lover back, but a real man; a solid entity. Not this – *ghost in the house.*

There. She had said it. There was a ghost in the house.

Her friend Leela knew priests. They would exorcise the ghost and she and Troy would be free of his father and her husband, forever and forever, and that would be the saddest thing that had ever happened to her, not given his death seven years ago.

The saddest thing. She wanted her husband without the history, without the drugs and the drinking, without the violence, without the mistresses.

Sometimes he was the sweetest man.

She loved that man, and the memory of him that glossed over his deficits and his failures, that had buried with him the thousand arrows of hurt he had inflicted in life, and smoothed with time the wrinkles and furrows of anger he had inflicted on her. He didn't respect nor even like women overmuch, that was for sure. Scarlett sighed. They were such a pair!

She loved him still.

Troy was silent in his room.

"Dear? Troy?" She tiptoed to the painted wooden door with the DO NOT ENTER sign on it; ear to the door and heard his robots marching and his giggle of delight. In the kitchen, the phone trilled again. This time she answered it.

Is Michael Kane there?

"Yes," she said and there was silence. She hung up.

She put her son to bed and sat by herself in the living room with the orange feature wall, the mahogany paneling, and the green shag rug. In the dark, great resolve coursed through her brain and into her gut, exploding in excitement at another day ahead to put plans into place and fix her own life - men, neighbors, and family be damned.

24

Scarlett didn't care that someone watched her from a corner. What had started the haunting, she didn't know, but felt that it was Michael's love for her and his son and his wish to protect them or watch over them. He was trapped because he cared too much, though in death. Especially in death. He, too, could not let go.

Her heart swelled with pride. And a plan.

A mouse scratched behind the walls. The mice had never left the walls in all this time, were impervious to traps, and Rocker Patch was a completely useless mouser, she thought. She kept him only because he had been Michael's and because her son loved him.

The cat licked daintily at its water bowl, stared at an invisible spot in the corner, and ignored the scratching behind the ivy-covered kitchen walls. He began to purr.

She shook her head and headed off to ready Troy's nightly shower and shampoo. A radio in the distance played "Born to be Wild" from Easy Rider. Coincidence? She didn't care.

* * *

When an engine coughed outside their home the next afternoon, she locked the doors and searched in the antique desk where odd scraps of paper and receipts were stuffed into cubbies. "I know I put his number somewhere. John Aguila at the corner store. Here it is."

She called John and asked him to deliver a mickey of cherry whiskey right away if he had one at home, and they would share it, and she would get drunk and be happy. Michael be damned. Troy came home, was fed and put to bed. She was such a bad mother! Memories of her sponsor Brian in AA urged her to "put the plug in the jug" but just this once she would be a rebel and take a chance. Perhaps she needed "liquid courage" to face her new plan.

It was a big risk that the old spiral would begin again into a haze of alcohol, but at this point she didn't care. Years had gone by since her last drink, and she had not been a lifelong alcoholic, after all. Surely it was due to circumstance. Yes, it may have been. Troy hardly remembered her drinking and, in any case, would be asleep in his bed tonight. She remembered John's kindnesses over the years, and his patience. Surely, it was time to enjoy a convivial drink with a companion. She hated being different or at least appearing different than others, her neighbors, her new friend.

Yes, cherry whiskey tonight and that would be all for the drinking until she could show she could handle it. An experiment, she thought, and that is all, but controlled in her own capable hands with assistance. John Aguila would help her over the test and not know he played a pivotal role. It was better that way, Scarlett assured herself, and her stomach fluttered in anticipation. After a cup of coffee while waiting, her heart palpitated, too, and so her face was flushed when John appeared.

"I've always thought you're beautiful," the shopkeeper murmured to the woman with the flower eyes when he arrived with the whiskey. "We're neighbors, after all. I'm so happy you called. If I can do anything for you, just let me know."

He put out a warm hand to place on hers. His hand felt sticky. She could see the dark hairs curling on the back of it. The ghost didn't come to the door or through the door after all, though as she half rose in her chair to look out the window, she caught a glimpse of a tall male figure around the corner. Perhaps Michael had learned his lesson and wouldn't appear. It was tit for tat, after all, she told herself. He had not been faithful in life and could not expect her to be faithful after his death. Ridiculous, really, to think she should be faithful to a dead man. Was it all a dream after all?

Scarlett hadn't cared overmuch for the shopkeeper at first, but he hung around hoping for more attention from her than she gave him, and she was too stuck in the past to make an end of it. As he could be useful to her, she also thought she *ought* to keep him around. She deserved more than a ghost from the abusive years of her brief marriage, and John was all there was. She was a bad friend but the merry widow!

"I hope this is only one more of many evenings together," John murmured, pouring the drinks. "I've admired you from the beginning. I think we can ease the loneliness together, can't we, my dear?"

This may have been a mistake. John Aguila was far too importunate. She sipped at the cherry whiskey and guiltily enjoyed the glow.

Rocker Patch, crouched near the stove, hissed at the shopkeeper. The lights flickered and crackled. The mice skittered and scratched behind the ivy-covered walls and fresh snow drifted behind the panes of glass. John's conversation as always was amusing and his attentiveness rewarding. She enjoyed the male companionship and relaxed.

John and Scarlett, with the presence of an invisible Michael, who after all flickered through locked doors, enjoyed the last glass of *bon vivant* for the night. Later, the shopkeeper leaned into the March weather and dashed home, full of optimism for something that could never be.

Because Scarlett loved Michael. He would always be there for her. She didn't have to worry about waiting for him in grief. He would wait for her. Michael would wait forever, behind the lace curtains and the automatons of their new home in Calder, far from old hurts and violences.

Scarlett smiled at the thought and her cheeks glowed. Tall and distinguished, and casting loving dusky glances behind him into the square of light in the porch with the woman silhouetted against it, John Aguila thought the glow was for him.

It was not.

Perhaps a true alcoholic would have relapsed more than Scarlett did on this occasion. She thought of her friends and Troy, and her own good health. She even laughed a little that night at the drink and her desire to get even with Michael by hurting herself. The haze lifted finally and she lay in bed, the walls and ceiling wheeled, and she called Brian at AA.

"The best revenge is living well," he said. "We're here for you."

There were no more "slips" and no more visits to AA even though her acquaintances there and Brian looked for her to return, crestfallen and drinking. She did not.

25

Michael appeared more often as a solid entity in Scarlett's house. His arms felt warm and firm, not as she remembered him in the bad times, but as she remembered the good times.

As years ago, when Troy was a baby, she now grew to recognize the sound of her husband's vehicle as it turned the corner. The whiskey had been a one-time slip, an occurrence she was not proud of and a slippery slope, but John was there to encourage her to quit, and the recent good solid side of Michael.

"Don't push it," Michael said. "You never drank at home, darling, until you reached rock bottom. Don't start again. Remember our son, and your pride, and my love."

He often parked his motorcycle in the driveway behind the leaning fence and the hedge. She would catch a glimpse of it at times, large and chromed, not the old Honda she remembered of course but a two-year-old Harley, with a passenger seat and a trunk.

"Take me for a ride sometime, Mike?" she murmured with her head on his broad shoulder.

"I don't trust the traffic," he replied, shaking his head. "It's not safe and I only have one helmet."

"I'll buy one," she urged.

He shrugged. "I don't take passengers."

"Why do you ride something that would kill you?"

"My spirit wants to die," he replied. "Please, Scarlett. Find a way to put my soul at rest."

"How do I do that? You're a ghost anyhow."

"I'm more real than you think. There are ways and I'll help you."

She tore herself from his arms and sat at the kitchen table. The light burned steadily from the ceiling. It flickered only during storms and at the times when Michael's psyche was like a storm. Not now, when he was calm and loving. She appreciated this side of him and wished it would last.

Alas, it never lasted, and he would be replaced soon by an apparition she could see through, with arms like cold mist, and the old mocking sneer in his voice intimating hatred and anger she could never understand but sometimes matched.

His lean arms folded, he sat across from her, and tilted back in the chrome chair. "You have to do something about the ghosts and the spirits that surround you and the boy."

"Your son, you mean?"

"Yes. He's vulnerable and the spirits are loathsome."

Scarlett frowned and pinched her lip. "But you're a spirit."

His chair crashed onto the shiny tiles. "Feel this. Feel my hands. Feel my arms and chest. I can embrace you. I am real."

"I don't understand what you're talking about. You were killed in a motorcycle crash in 1971, when Troy was only three years old. There was a hole in the back of your head, I saw you in the coffin. I was there when you were buried.

"You're a ghost, Michael, and I never wanted this, but now that you're back, I don't know that I want you gone, either. There seem to be two sides of you, the loving and warm and the other that I remember so well, the ghost that sneers at my frailty and casts fire into my soul."

He sighed and moved away from her, scraping his chair as he did so, then moved it back with a bang. "I know. It's confusing. For old time's sake, Scarlett, let's pretend I never died. Let's have a day of love."

"We used to, sometimes, very rarely, then you'd leave and come home again very late and in a bad mood."

"I regretted it immediately."

"You told the doctor you'd failed. That's all it was. You'd failed and not that you had hurt me."

"My mother…"

She catapulted to her feet. "Damn your mother! She did this to you, I know she did, but that's not to say you should spend the rest of your life ruminating about it or that I should suffer for her abuse. Where are your balls, Mike?"

He hung his head. "Let's have a day together, darling. Like we used to."

"Yes, there were good times, so confusing, because they had no connection to the bad times. I hated you, Michael. You knew that?"

"Yes."

"I loved you, too. How can that be? I was a wreck, and any amount of marriage counseling only made it worse. The therapist Lawrence blamed me!"

"He was judgmental and unfair."

"You said you loved him. Was that right? He wanted in your pants, Michael!"

The solid apparition on the other side of the table winced. "I was very ill."

Scarlett threw up her hands. "You don't take responsibility."

Michael scraped his chair back again and rose to his feet. He strode to the other side of the kitchen and back. "I don't want to leave us this way," he said. He wiped a hand over his face. "I'll be back, probably tonight, and there's nothing I can do about it. Think about getting help, dear, and please put my soul at rest. You have the capability. You just have to let go."

"I know. I can't let go."

"Please. Let him – me – go."

She got up, too, and approached him. "You won't leave me. You'll never leave me. But believe me, Mike, I have a plan."

"The potions, the crystals are no good if your spirit hangs onto me."

"I think I know what you want."

He nodded. "What I've always wanted. I want love, Scarlett, I'm begging you for love. It's been missing for so long. Only true love can let go and believe it will be okay."

"Yes. You needed my love in life and I couldn't give it wholeheartedly. Lawrence was right, in that respect, we were two people who had never known a lot of affection, and the personalities he gave us because he thought we were so dysfunctional were wrong. He put us together wrong."

"It would have been best to start over, my love. Like now."

"We can't start over. Too much baggage. Now you seem clear of the baggage I remember, Michael. You seem to be clear-headed and I can trust your vision. I long to let go. To be free. But I don't want to let go of the good times. I don't know if you want me to."

"I'm begging you," he said. "The apparition needs the love he was denied in life, and he'll be satisfied. You have to let go of the spirit that dug into you in life, the wrong that Lawrence and our experiences planted in us both. The clouds of hate and anger, the confusion, they'll all clear up. It isn't fair to Troy to live in a house of ghosts and his father's spirit. He knows his father died and he's confused by spirits and ghosts. You, most of all, confuse and confound him."

Hugging her goodbye, her husband left out the door as a normal man. She heard the Harley chug out of her driveway and then roar down the street. She pressed her face to the frosted front window. A blast of dark smoke lingered in the cold afternoon air.

"He took time off work to tell me that," she mused then slapped herself playfully on the side of her head. "Work, shlurk, he doesn't work anymore and the middle of the day is like night to him. Crazy woman I am. This is not a real man."

* * *

Troy's birthday was next month in April. Scarlett planned nothing for it but a family gathering, a cake she made from scratch, and a magnificent gift for the young boy. Better than a baseball glove.

She knew the best gift she could give her son was to let go of the past and let go of the ghost that was his father roaming the rooms of their little house where she had hoped to escape their dark history.

Sometimes Scarlett thought she might be schizoid. It was a possibility.

26

John Aguila's tall form, comfortably sturdy, strode to the back porch of Scarlett's house, alongside the cotoneaster hedge covered now with more early March snow and rustling with a northeast wind.

He snatched the tuque from his head and bowed somewhat as Scarlett answered the door. "I brought you a jar of cream for the cat and a bottle of milk. Do you want a jar of yogurt, too? I notice the little guy likes it."

She threw the door open. "Come in before the cold gets into the kitchen," she said, brushing her nutbrown hair back from her forehead. "No, we don't need yogurt at this time but he does like it with honey and berries. A little healthy treat. Next time we're at the grocery store I'll get some. I don't want you to be inconvenienced from the convenience store, convenient though it is," and she grinned.

He smiled and shrugged his woolen jacket off his broad shoulders. He set the bottles on the kitchen table next to the entryway.

Rocker Patch meandered across the room from his litterbox

in the hallway. The orange cat didn't hiss but rubbed its cheeks on John's ankles and purred.

One hand on the doorknob in the small kitchen, the store owner pulled up a chair with the other and lifted a dark eyebrow to question whether it was okay to sit.

"Yes, John, do sit down. It's an ugly night to be out, even for such a short distance as your place to mine. Hard to believe it will be spring in two weeks."

"Yes, you know what they say about March and the lion. I didn't want to leave the milk outside in the cold to maybe freeze," he explained, and clasped his big hands under his chin as he gazed at the beautiful woman. "Also, you know, I wanted to see you. Troy is in bed or can I say goodnight to him?"

"No, he's in bed but probably not asleep yet. I'd rather not disturb him, though. You know what they say about sleeping puppies. Rocker's on his way to his bed, I expect. He sleeps with Troy."

John reached down and stroked the marmalade cat behind its ears. Rocker Patch responded by curling around the man's ankles and purring. "Cream?" John asked.

"Actually, it's not good for him," Scarlett replied. "But maybe a little. He does like it."

Cream was poured for the cat in a little white dish. He lapped the thick rich treat and then dipped a pink paw into the dish and licked it. When the dish was empty, he again brushed his cheek against John's leg, marking the man for his own, then padded off to slip into Troy's room. John and Scarlett watched him go.

"You should get a furry pet," Scarlett observed. "You're good with them."

"I'd like to," said John, "but I travel for part of the winter when I shut down the store, to get away from the cold and dark here in Alberta. I'd either have to take a pet with me or board it, and it wouldn't be fair to the cat or dog."

"You do have birds, though? There's at least two or three in that bronze bell-shaped cage in your store."

"Yes, I have the opaline and green budgies. They don't seem to breed, so I suspect they're all one gender or else they want their privacy. I leave them with my mother when I go away. She likes the company and they're not a lot of bother for her."

"I've never met your mother."

"I'll introduce you sometime. We don't always get along," he said. "She's a feisty old person, as my father was in his time. He passed away of heart troubles about ten years ago, but my mother continues in the house they shared in the Bonnie Doon area, quite a long distance from here. She doesn't get out much anymore. Quite frail now and quit driving a few years ago, after my dad died."

Scarlett smiled politely. "I'd like to meet her sometime. Why don't you get along?"

"Oh, she thinks I ought to have married and supplied grandchildren a long time ago. She thinks I have no ambition. I did well in school and have a college certificate in business, but she doesn't recognize the store as an entrepreneurship or a success. I'm sure I disappoint the cantankerous old Spaniard."

"We often feel that way about our parents," she commented. "Tea?"

"Why not?" he asked, and got up to put the kettle on the burner.

"You've been here enough to know your way around," she observed. "I should probably offer you something stronger."

"Oh, no, thanks, I think the whiskey was a mistake. Tea will be fine." When the kettle boiled, Scarlett tipped the bubbling liquid into a pretty English teapot and put out chocolate squares.

Now that they were again seated, he reached across the table for a square. "You're a good cook."

She raised her brows. "Practice. Not as good as your meat-loaf, though."

"My only specialty," he laughed. Some crumbs dropped onto his lap. He dabbed at them with a white paper napkin. "What about you, Scarlett? I never hear you talk about your family other than Michael and Troy. Where were you born?"

Her hands trembled as she tore a piece of cake. She shifted in her chair. "Here in Alberta. Not much to say. Unlike you, I'm not an only child, have two brothers and three sisters, but like you, my parents were disappointed in me, though they attended our wedding in 1965. It was a small wedding. We weren't sure they would come. They gave us a wonderful leather recliner for a gift, I remember, which was a surprise. They live up north near Fort St. John and have a small farm there, though they plan to retire soon and divide the farm between my two brothers.

"My brothers are both bachelors. It's an isolated community and they don't get away much. The oldest boy, Ben, is quite a grump like my father, but the other, Patrick, is happy-go-lucky enough and we all thought he'd marry young, but he surprised us. My sisters all married young and moved away, probably to get away from the farm and its demands. A lot of hard work there and little appreciation from my father."

"He sounds rather dour. Scot?"

"No, our great-grandparents settled in Ontario in the 1800s so we're third or fourth generation Canadian. Mixed extraction – I really don't know what to call us children. My mother's English and German and my father's family was Polish, originally from the Red Ruthenia region, only partially in modern Poland now. His great grandfather was Prussian, I think."

"Ah, a Teutonic temperament."

"Yes, but he loved a good joke. I remember he beamed at me constantly. I think I was his favorite. My siblings are older than me. Ben is the oldest and Patrick is one of the middle children. We girls are all over the place. I think really my father wanted a family of boys to help on the farm."

"Girls can help on the farm. I know many farm wives and daughters who worked alongside the men as hard as the men worked."

She shrugged and poured more tea. "Yes, but our family wasn't like that. We girls helped in the garden and with the chickens, and we baked and cooked and did housework."

"Yuck," he said.

"I know. I rebelled, and thus the disappointment. I didn't marry well, either, but I don't think they suspected that. I remember my mother telling me after Michael had managed to subjugate me within a couple of years, that I was a 'good girl.'"

"Ugh." He stirred milk into his cup of steaming Red Rose tea. "Where's the miniatures that come in the box of Red Rose tea?"

"A nice change of topic," she laughed, relieved, and reached across to the windowsill where all sorts of Wade miniatures shone in the electric light. "Here they are."

"Of course," he said. "My mother collects them, too."

She reached across the table and took John's hand. "You know, John, we can't ever be more than friends. You're a good friend and I value your company. I miss you when you're gone to Comox in January and February, and I appreciate your kindness. Troy looks up to you, too. But I hope I'm not leading you on."

"No," he said. "I know you're right and I understand. I think Troy's a fine young man and I would be proud to be part of your family. But there just isn't the spark there for you. I know I'm a plain fellow. I've always been plodding. I think you're as fair as a lily of the valley, Scarlett. I admit I desired you from the moment I saw you walk into my store but there's the age difference, too."

"Thank you, John. Every summer holiday I take Troy to see

his father's grave in the Beechmount Cemetery. He has a flat stone, red granite, simply says Rest in Peace. I thought it was appropriate. We're going to skip it this summer, but you're welcome to join us there any other time. You've heard enough about him."

"You used to live in that area, didn't you? Near 124th Avenue and 104th Street?"

"Our house was near the Municipal Airport where we could almost see the pilot's eyes as they roared over our roof," laughed Scarlett. "Cheap rent because of it. Our friend Nancy Clarke still lives in that area, with our parakeet Max and our dog Angus."

John Aguila wiped his mouth with the paper napkin. He reached for another chocolate confection. "This will be the last square and the last cup of tea for today. Delicious." He patted his stomach. The sleeves of his loose cotton sweater were rolled up to his elbows. She couldn't avoid noting the knotted muscles underneath his forearms, covered with dark hairs. She wondered how she would react if he pressed her body to his muscular chest. *No.*

Michael was so real to her, solid and loving as he had been last night. She had no room for another man in her heart, and she wished moreover for the chemistry that sparkled between her and Michael when he was as loving as he had been last night, and his face smoothed of the habitual sneer and the tone of his voice calm and gentle, as it was all too seldom. Last night had been magical.

"I don't have a chance," commented John, and she started with the accuracy of his observation at just this time.

"We're good friends, though," she said. "There'll be someone out there for you, John. You're an attractive man, just a little shy around women until you get to know us."

"Yeah." He rose and pulled on his woolen jacket, bunching the collar up over his ears. When she opened the door for him, the northeast wind had picked up in intensity and whipped snow into the grey porch. A snow shovel leaned against the inside wall and a broom. He grasped the broom and swept the four inches of snow onto the sifting white drifts in the backyard.

"Don't forget your hat," she called and he grinned and waved as he ran down the steps. "Thanks!

"Thanks for the tea and treats," he called back. "Good time to be going home. This storm is blowing in from the Arctic Circle and I think it's going to settle for a week or more. Take care, Scarlett, and make sure Troy bundles up warm tomorrow." His strong baritone voice was almost lost in the howl of the blizzard.

"What?" she screamed into the gale, but he had gone, his form illuminated only by a streetlight swept by blowing snow.

"Darn country," Scarlett muttered and pulled the door shut onto the warmth and silence of her home. The electric bulb in the kitchen ceiling dimmed. "Damn." The temperature dropped by five degrees, which sometimes happened before the *ghost in the house* made its entrance. The mice scratched and skittered behind the walls but no apparition appeared.

"He's sulking and jealous," she laughed and felt good about it. If only she could keep the good parts and discard the rest. A plan formed in her mind as she prepared to let go of the past and the spirit that haunted her little home.

27

The ruby birthstone ring Scarlett buried her husband with was not after all lost to the perfidy of the funeral directors. During his short, reckless life she believed the precious gem protected him from harm. The violent motorcycle crash in the summer of 1971 tore all hope of redemption of the man and marriage from her.

A gift that burned in the blackness of his soul, the ring sparkled now from his ghost's right middle finger but she noticed it was not always present. It had never been more than an ornament in life, a love token unappreciated but worn from duty and perhaps a sense of pride and a flicker of love. She had given him the ring on his birthday two years before their wedding, two months after they first met in a fever, hotter than a chili pepper.

Scarlett leafed through the stack of ephemerides listing the motions of the stars and planets at the time of Michael's birth in August 1942 and her own in October 1944. He liked being a Leo, the lion, the captain of his soul and hers. Despite Dorothy's insistence that astrology was bunk, Scarlett believed the stars that no longer swung in the exact synchronicity as today across the astrological heavens were still powerful millennia after the zodiac was created.

She believed in the power of crystals and precious gems, in the power of the ruby even though it was unproven. In the power of first love.

Her creations on the worktable tick-tocked and refuted Michael's disbelief that his wife could construct an automaton capable of encapsulating his spirit. She had in mind a sort of exorcism, but wasn't sure it would work unless she truly let go of his spirit with hers. She felt she was ready. She engaged her son in this new endeavor and, as a result, his father's final ordeal and deliverance.

Troy's mechanical robots marched toward the construction that was his father. Gears whirred and the winding keys in the back turned slowly beneath the bobbing mechanical heads and the glaring flashlight eyes.

"How wondrously and fearsomely we are made," Scarlett expostulated, as her husband's form writhed in the grip of the mechanical structures and chants that captured his soul. The six-inch steel figures whirled along the metal track created by her son, stretching across the dusty olefin basement floor to the corner where Michael's scaffolded body afforded the creatures a foothold to climb to his brain.

He retched at the turpentine-balsamic odor of the bubbling liquid in the Erlenmeyer flask controlled by the clockworks of Scarlett's machinations with black iron pipes and lamp parts on the worktable.

"We've got him now," cried Troy and tipped the first of the six-inch steel robots up toward the long expanse of his father's torso to his brain.

Michael's mouth distorted into a smile behind the lattice-work of metal that enveloped his face. Wisps of smoke escaped from his ears. Green ectoplasm oozed from the sides of his eyes. Naked except for a pair of Oilers hockey team boxer shorts, a gift his wife remembered from their second Christmas together, Michael attempted to speak.

"I'm your father," the figure wheezed and he continued to grin; reached out to pat the curls on his son's head. "You've proven yourself far beyond me, Troy Michael Kane. How many years is it from your birth that I missed?

"I'm so sorry, Scarlett. You don't deserve these visitations any more than you deserved the treatment I gave you both when I was alive. But my resurrection was needed for my own redemption and yours."

The robots continued their inexorable climb to his head where his brain hung exposed in the back of a gaping skull held together only by the metal cage. She crossed the room and put her hand on the fatty grey organ. "You've been hiding your wound," she whispered.

Michael's ghost wheezed and green ectoplasm swirled from his mouth into the room. The last of the robots chuffed to the top of the scaffolding around Michael's head. The flask bubbled and squealed on the Bunsen burner. Made visible by bright beams of sunlight through the high window, murky liquid swirled and dissipated as gas in the dusty air of the basement. The cotoneaster's glossy oval leaves were beginning to green in the yard outside.

Preparing to dig, the robots wielded their sharp instruments onto Michael's damp flesh. He began to laugh. The ectoplasm swirled and formed sluggishly into a familiar form.

28

"My old friend Scott's mom?" Troy asked in disbelief as Scarlett gasped.

Remembered fondly from seven years ago, their friend Nancy from their former neighborhood swayed by Michael's side.

The mechanical clockworks whirred, the steel track hummed as the robots hesitated and the Erlenmeyer flask fractured and fell to the floor. Lastly, Nancy's face took better shape. She stood average height and stocky, hazel eyes warm and kind as Scarlett remembered her.

"Stop!" Troy commanded the robots and pressed a button. The six-inch mechanical beings sheathed their instruments and marched down again on the long track across the scaffolding to the floor and back to Troy's feet.

The crystals Scarlett held stirred in her palm. She knew the ruby worn on her husband's right finger held a magic far more powerful than any stones she possessed, although it had not protected him from physical harm in the end. The latticework clattered from around Michael's spirit body and his soul shone forth, the hole in the back of his head no longer evident. The lustrous mop of blond hair curled around his neck.

Troy ran to his father and threw his arms around his waist. They connected with solid flesh. The robots lay in a heap in the middle of the room. Michael, awkward as always with physical touch, stroked his son's head and his cheeks were wet with salty spiritual tears.

"I have a heart," he whispered. His form grew soft in outline and his smile melted onto the corners of his lips and began to bend the beautiful full mouth.

"What are *you* doing here, Nancy?" gasped Scarlett. She moved away from the pair who stood incorporeally before her, the glass on the photograph behind them glinting and reflecting into her eyes.

"My spirit was always here with him, in the background, invisible. My body remains at home where you knew me," Nancy whispered. "I have a message for you.

Ruby, Stone of Fire and Sun, I activate you with Love,
Protect me from the Right, Left, Below and Above!"

Scarlett shook her head. "I don't understand."

"This beautiful gem, the stone of the planet Mars and the astrological sign Leo, maintains and enhances wisdom, wealth, and keeps away evil witches and evil wizards.

"Your husband's ring also came to him in death from the physical world to the spiritual world and protected him in hell from the fate he deserved. Because it was a powerful love token blessed by innocence."

"What do *you* have to do with my husband?" demanded Scarlett. She tore her son from Michael's embrace and placed her arms around the boy.

"Isn't it obvious, darling?" asked Nancy. "My spirit flew here on command of the crystals you hold.

"I knew you needed me after all these years, as you needed me when we were neighbors. My body is corporeal and waits as usual in the little house you remember, with my son Scott who was Troy's best friend in our old neighborhood. My spirit flew to Michael and you because it was summoned but I am as you remember me in life.

"This spirit you see is but an astral projection. Surely you understand that, my friend. We were close and remain close. My spirit mourns with you even though I betrayed you. I pray that you forgive me."

"But who *are* you to my husband?" Scarlett asked. Troy held tightly to his mother's hand. "What do you mean you betrayed me?"

"I was his mistress," Nancy admitted, thrusting out her chin.

"But the secretary..."

Michael put his arm around Nancy's shoulders. "A ruse," he said. "You never would have suspected your good friend and neighbor, and it was easier to blame a co-worker."

Scarlett screamed a long primal scream, then covered her mouth. Eyes wide, gaping at his father, Troy put both hands over his ears and ran to the doorway then back to his mother.

Michael held out a hand to Scarlett. "I'm sorry," he said. "I can explain."

"What?" gasped Scarlett. "Explain what?"

"Dad!" Troy gasped. A tall lanky man with pale hair and cerulean blue eyes leaned against the doorway behind him. Scarlett's gaze darted from him to the form in the corner. She could not tell the difference between the two figures, except *her* Michael was almost naked and bruised, and faint wisps of smoke trailed from the openings in his face. He stood with one arm around Nancy and a hand outstretched toward Scarlett.

29

"Michael's an identical twin," Nancy said. "His brother's name is Charles. He has been waiting for you and his brother's son. Charles is real and solid in this world, Scarlett. He will comfort you with the same arms that comforted you in the past, if you'll allow it."

"I left home when I was in my late teens," said Michael. Nancy's astral body snuggled closer to him.

"I was always the black sheep and Charles was the good guy. We agreed that we would keep in touch secretly, because our parents didn't want anything more to do with me. Rightfully so, as you know, Scarlett, rightfully so. I was a bad seed from the beginning. Charles seemed to get all the good that should have been shared between us.

"Charles shared in my marriage with you, though you didn't know it. I know it was wrong but he protected me when I needed an alibi. Even at my funeral, when he was absent so you wouldn't know the subterfuge, he had an excuse for our parents. Watching my back and yours was his obsession for years. The scratching and the lights in Troy's room? That was my ghost, uneasy, searching for my son and his little soul, unable to rest. The man peering through the curtains was Charles, looking after you, making sure it was okay, putting my spirit at arm's length so I wouldn't hurt my family any more than I already had."

The man lounging against the doorsill took a few steps into the room. "It was very wrong," he said. "I'm so sorry. I wanted to protect you from my brother's wrongdoing and give you a little of the life I wanted you to have."

"There were *two* of you?" gasped Scarlett. "I know my husband was unpredictable – sometimes sweet; sometimes uncaring. But I didn't ever suspect – *this*. How could you get away with such a secret, such a huge lie all these years?"

"Michael has always been very manipulative," his brother said. "You were young and trusting. It was easy for him to do."

Scarlett frowned, straightened, reached out her slim arms, and hugged Troy even tighter. "Why have you come back? Stay away from my son."

"I fell in love with you," Charles said simply. He shrugged and hooked his thumbs into the big belt buckle.

"Did you – did you ever...?"

"No," Charles said. "I never touched you. Not in that way."

"We respected you too much for that," Michael said.

"Did you ever love me, Michael?" asked Scarlett. Troy tore himself from Scarlett's arms and ran past his uncle and out the door. They could hear his footsteps on the stairs going out.

"I loved you dearly," her husband said.

Nancy nodded. "That is true."

"Why did you treat me that way?" Scarlett queried. She felt sick to her stomach. "Can someone get my son?" she continued.

Charles turned and disappeared toward the stairs. They heard the back door open and close and his voice, so familiar, calling to Troy.

"There's a song by Johnny Cash about a snake who bit a woman who rescued it," replied Nancy. "The snake said, as she was dying, 'You knew I was a snake when you took me in.' It was his nature."

Scarlett's head reeled. Voices and footsteps on the stairs heralded the return of Troy and Charles.

"A bad seed," she murmured.

"I tried to make it up to you," Michael replied. "But it was obvious to me that it was Charles you loved. And he loved you."

"Why didn't you tell me?"

Michael hung his head. "I was protecting myself. I was afraid. There was so much to lose, especially after we had a son."

She thought back to that dreadful day. "Then the bike. Then the rain and the bridge and the light standard. The accident. Where were you going that night? Nancy was home all the time. I know because I talked to her in the morning."

Michael shook his head. The ectoplasm that was Nancy's spirit moaned, connected to her body restless and real in her bed in the old house. Like a wolf with a knife to its bones, she wailed and screamed a song that struck her former friend's soul. *Jolene.*

30

Scarlett's chakras caught fire and electric shocks raced up and down her spine. She spilled the crystals from her other hand onto the floor, where they clattered and shone like little diamonds, like precious gems which they were not. Some of them shone as rubies should.

"He was unfaithful to me, too," said Nancy. "He had an assignation on the south side with his secretary from the company he worked for."

"So, there *was* a secretary involved."

"Yes. I knew it, too. And I loved him - the wild man, the cruel man, the husband of my best friend.

"Until I'm freed by my conscience and you, I must suffer eternally in this form, tied to Michael's spirit. I'm going through the motions of living back in our old neighborhood, Scarlett. Where you may still find me, if you wish."

"We weren't such good friends that we kept in touch," declared Scarlett. "Perhaps it was guilt on your part that kept us apart after we moved to Calder, despite our bird Max and my dog Angus who must have reminded you constantly of us?"

"Guilt and grief," replied Nancy's spirit. "Still I mourn in the lonely little rooms that should have been vacated or renovated years ago. Our spirits have come to make restitution, as the laws of the universe decree. My Jack left me long ago for the open road and other arms."

"I'm sorry," Scarlett said. "He left you long before that, I know. And I – I never came back for Angus or Max, and I never missed them, nor did I miss you, my friend, so deep in my suffering I was.

"Somewhere in all of us there is an empty shell that should have been filled with love for all God's creatures, but instead, selfishness and isolation from all that is good and warm in this world, all that would make us complete – male and female, or each gender with its own. All so alone and longing for companionship and love."

Michael reached out and touched his wife's arm. "I am dead," he said. "I won't return. Make a new life with Charles and our son. Be happy, wife. That's what I always wished for you. I couldn't help myself, Scarlett. I sometimes think I was too ill to control my own actions."

"He *couldn't* control his actions." Michael's twin stood in the doorway again, his arm around Troy. "He was too weak."

"Charles got all the good genes." Michael's gaze fell on the boy then on his wife. "I am so sorry, Scarlett."

"I'm sorry, too," Charles said. "I've waited all these years for you to let go. But I couldn't make myself known. I look just like him. But I'm not a ghost, Scarlett. I'm real."

"But *why?*" gasped Scarlett, throwing her arms behind her onto the worktable. "Why would you deceive me so?"

An engine began to chuff, put in motion by the tilt of the table. The reason for building the streamlined mechanism became clear. It lurched at the end of the track, metal wings stretching out from the cast iron steam tanks, and ploughed upward through the ether dragging her husband's immortal soul past the old ceiling beams, locked in the churning liquid from the Erlanger flask upturned on the floor, with the witch's spell screaming and ascending to what her neighbor Leela ever after insisted was Purgatory, where his soul would be cleansed.

Michael screamed as he ascended in smoke and grease. The spring green oval cotoneaster leaves skittered and whirled in a sudden storm outside the paned window glass – then the eye of the storm became very still. The red sky vanished from the square of glass above their heads. Darkness covered the landscape like a huge flapping crow.

"I am fierce now," Scarlett spoke. "Not like you remember, Michael."

"Good on you, my dear." His form wavered. He and Nancy's translucent spirit held hands. Both shone like a moonbeam on snow, cold and white and lucid.

Scarlett put a finger underneath her chin and frowned. "Wait a minute, Nancy."

"What is it, dear?" As milk flows from an udder when squeezed, the words oozed from Nancy's form.

"The phone calls. Was that you?" Michael looked confused. The shining ectoplasm that was Nancy's soul shuddered.

"Yes. It wasn't my body, dear. Understand, I love you and Troy very much. It was my spirit, reaching out, lost, lonely into electronic hell just to hear a human voice speak his name in this world."

"Hoping to hurt me," Scarlett accused. She smashed a fist on the table. "Cruel, unusual, too weird, Nancy. How could you? Don't you know it frightened and disgusted us?"

"I know. I'm so sorry. It was the only way I could bring even a semblance of being to my amorphous soul here on Earth. One day my spirit slipped in through a crack in Troy's window. Do you remember, the phone would not ring late at night? That night it did."

"Why?" Scarlett asked.

The cold silver moonlight in the room hardened to pure

agony then darkened with cloud heralding a coming storm. "Anger. Hatred. Hurt. You hurt Michael, you know. Part of me was torn apart at that as well as what I did to cope with the spoiled marriages between the two of us. Jack, my absent husband, and Michael, your handsome infidel who sought me out with his tales of marital unhappiness."

Scarlett considered. "Yes. I know he did that with many vulnerable women, and some believed him. I wasn't able to defend myself, beaten down as I was, and with a child and a society who blames the wife for the husband's behavior. Some day I hope that changes. I will be the first to advocate for single mothers and abused wives."

"My soul will leave your house now, my friend. Please forgive me the trespass. I was very lonely and very unhappy."

"As you deserve to be, Nancy," Scarlett snapped. "I forgive you and I'm sorry I didn't seek you out after we moved to Calder. You took care of Angus and Max for me, you loved me and my son in your way, and you were always there for me, no matter what the circumstances of your alternative life. I know that you gave Michael what I could not - although, my dear, his secretary probably gave him more!"

"The secretary. Yes, the mystery element who might have stood at the fringes of the funeral and laughed at us."

"Or not."

The shards of light in the room displaced Nancy's form and clicked like a kaleidoscope. "We don't know. There's so much of heaven and hell right here on Earth that people create for themselves. We lonely women have certainly lain ourselves down in many a bedroom, like the poets of old."

Nancy's spirit fractured and split into thousands of silver flakes. It whisked away as the eye of the storm shifted and held her briefly in its icy embrace. The photograph of Botticelli's Eighth Circle of Hell which hung on the basement wall opposite the worktable, enshrined by the glass that glared and glimmered on so many occasions to blind them, crashed to the floor and shattered. Hovering above the ceiling of solid wood but somehow through it, Scarlett's husband and his mistress smiled in anticipation of grace.

A biplane that had been an automaton leading to his brain soared into a swirling bank of cloud. Scarlett forever remembered his parting words. "Please forgive me."

"Forgive me, too," she called, and his soul ascended. "I forgive you, Nancy."

Michael and his female companion disappeared separately, he to a higher plane and Nancy's spirit back to her old house with her son Scott. She returned to memories of her faithless absent husband Jack and the wrongdoing she had to live with.

31

"It must have been torture for them," Scarlett said. "All those years of deceit and lovelessness at home."

"Yes. For you, too, don't forget. But it's over now. And I'm here if you want me," Charles whispered. Troy looked at his uncle with huge trusting eyes filled with tears.

"It will take some time. Perhaps forever," Scarlett said. She reached for her son and he leaned against her warm body.

"One thing, Charles. Michael worked for Coral Bay Oil & Gas Inc. for many years when I knew him. He loved it. It suited him though he didn't make a lot of money but he had good benefits and a good insurance policy. Which helped us so much. But you don't appear to have the means to make a living. What do you do?"

"I flip Fortune 500 businesses." Charles turned toward the door. "It's important to me to make my own hours and be able to be independent. I make a good living, be assured of that.

"I have good benefits too, Scarlett. A good insurance policy. Just like Michael. I can take good care of you and the boy, when you're ready. I only ask you to think about it. For now."

"Oh, sorry," Scarlett breathed. She put a hand on his arm. "I didn't mean to pry, Charles. But you seem to come and go like a ghost, too."

Charles smiled. "I do. I'm used to it. I'll leave now."

Troy reached out a hand. "No, don't go," he said. "You look just like dad."

"Give it time," Charles replied. His handsome face blossomed into a smile that was like a golden light in the dim doorway. His broad shoulders strained against the white cowboy shirt he wore and the enormous Western belt buckle hung low on his tight jeans. Scarlett's mouth was dry.

"I don't remember you other than the caring side of Michael," she said. "But I think we've saved my husband."

"I was part of the good times," Charles replied. "I can be again. I can be trusted, sweetheart."

"Yes," she said. "Good times will return."

Charles hugged her. The ghost of Michael's smile lingered in the warmth of his twin's.

"I love you," he whispered.

"I know, Charles. I've always loved you, too. It's too soon, though." She laughed. "Why don't you buy a candle? Party Lite makes the best candles!"

"I will be happy buying candles from you."

Scarlett shook her head. "Sounds depressing if that's all you do."

Troy giggled.

"Darling, we forgot you're listening. Little pitchers have big ears, my mother used to say."

"It's all right, Scarlett. Let him know this man loves you."

She took his hand. "So, you're the good bits that made me stay."

"I am. Let's talk about it later after the shock wears off. I can go away for a while."

She shook her head. "It's too much to comprehend right now. I don't even want to think about it."

"Don't think," he advised. "It's better that way."

32

"I'm really concerned about Scarlett and that young boy of hers," Karin Sivertsen whispered to her husband, Victor. Their fraternal twin sons, Eric and Jordan, played in the next room. "It's a wonderful thing what Penny and James are doing with him, taking him to church with them every Sunday and introducing him to new friends. He and Stevie Cardinal are thick as treacle. It's not that neither of them has other friends. They do.

"But she's so isolated there on that side of the street and she keeps him isolated, too. I swear they both look scared sometimes when they come out of that house. None of us knows what's going on. John from the store visits and he seems to be the only visitor she has, apart from that handsome Swedish looking fellow on the motorcycle and us four ladies from the neighborhood.

"And who is the biker? Nobody knows."

"I wouldn't worry about it, Karin," replied Victor. "It's none of our business. And Troy does fine in school, I think. As you say, he has friends. They just want to keep to themselves.

Nothing wrong with that, or with having a couple of male friends if you're a single young widow."

Karin sighed and plunked herself down on the orange Danish modern couch. She put her feet up on the cocktail table and leafed through a MAD magazine that belonged to one of their boys. "Funny," she said and chuckled.

"What?"

"The MAD 'Star Wars Musical' from December. Funny. Our boys loved Star Wars. Remember?"

"Remember? I took them to see it at least five times!"

"Better you than me."

"It was great," Victor said and strode to the kitchen, opened their Frigidaire and popped the top off a bottle of Liberty Ale his brother-in-law had brought across the American border because of the beer lockout in B.C. "Damn shortage. Damn unions," he said and tipped the bottle up to his lips. "Including mine."

"It's not their fault," Karin said mildly, flipping pages. In the next room, their boys raised their voices. "Uh-oh. Fight."

"Let them have at it," Victor advised. He sat beside her. "Anyhow, Kare, have we decided that our neighbors are none of our business?"

"I guess so, dear. If you say so," Karin murmured. "But it's Troy's birthday next week and we all have a little surprise planned."

He put down the bottle. "Oh-oh. What is it?"

"Stevie Cardinal came up with it. Troy will be eleven on April 4th. His mom is planning a quiet dinner and cake for the two of them," she said.

He wiped his mouth with a red handkerchief. "Nice."

She chuckled. He smoothed the black mohair sweater she wore and patted her back. "You're a good friend."

"Scarlett is a friend to all of us. Troy is very special. They shouldn't be alone on his birthday."

"What do your buddies say about that?"

She raised her eyebrows and smiled. Her lips were a shade of punchy coral and her face remained suntanned from last summer. He leaned over to kiss her but was interrupted by a crash in the next room.

Startled, their heads jerked around to the right. The twins came running into the family room, which was decorated in Hawaiian style. Eric got caught in a fishing net and another large conch shell crashed to the floor. Victor roared at the boys as they fell onto the couch and Karin sighed, flipping the magazine pages shut.

"Okay. What broke?"

Eric groaned. "It wasn't my fault, dad. He did it!"

"Did not!" Jordan punched him on the chest.

"Did so!"

"Stop it, boys! Let's go see the damage. The subject of our neighbors is closed for now."

Eric pushed his brother and responded, "What neighbors?"

"Just as well," Karin said. "I'm telling secrets out of school."

* * *

April 4, 1979

Scarlett whipped off her floral apron and brought the Black Forest cake to the table. "Ta-da!" she said.

Troy grinned. "Looks good, mom. Is John coming?"

"I didn't exactly invite anybody," she replied. "I thought we could celebrate, just the two of us. And Rocker, of course."

"Of course."

"He was always your father's cat, you know. I don't think he feels comfortable with me."

"He likes me. And he likes John."

Scarlett pursed her velvety orange lips. "That's true. He warmed up to John."

The boy patted his mother on the shoulder. "He likes you, too, mom."

"I don't know. Are you ready to eat? We have your favorite here. A big pan of lasagna."

"Oh, boy!"

"And garlic toast."

Troy smiled. "My favorites."

The back doorbell rang. Scarlett got up, placing her cloth napkin beside her plate. "Now who can that be at this time? It's dinnertime; everyone should know that."

33

When Scarlett opened the back door, she gasped to see her son's friend Stevie Cardinal standing on the old grey planks of the porch.

"Mrs. Kane! Is Troy home?"

She put a hand to her heart. "Why, Stevie! How nice. Yes, he is. Troy? It's for you, dear." Troy rose and strode to the door.

"Can you come out?" Stevie asked, brushing his long hair back. His large tinted glasses reflected Troy's pleased face.

"We're just eating," Troy explained. "Come in!"

The yard exploded with children. They came out from behind the leaning old fence; they came out from behind the cotoneaster hedge covered with a sprinkling of snow. The Cardinals and Balakrishnans and the Sivertsens, compatriots from the Foursquare Gospel Church, classmates from both schools – Scarlett's little house could barely hold them all.

They crowded into the kitchen and overflowed into the hallway, the living room with the orange wall and the Greek key gold couch, they crowded into Troy's room and some of them ended up in the basement in Scarlett's workshop, oohing and ahhing at the little engines and the mechanical wonders there, the crystals, the accoutrements of magic and ghosts which they did not comprehend.

Troy slapped his face with both hands and hooted when he realized that his friends had not forgotten him.

"Have some food, children," urged Scarlett, bringing out sausage, cheese, crackers, cookies, and chips. She poured big glasses of grape Kool-Aid and cut the cake into slices, procuring from the pantry paper plates and plastic cutlery.

"Wow, Mrs. Kane, you really know how to throw a party." Stevie smiled, adjusting his tinted lenses. All the children had brought brightly wrapped gifts: G.I. Joes, a plastic Slinky, a red yo-yo, Mattel's 1970s classic green Slime, a Battleship board game, science books, and Legos.

Troy opened each gift with reverence, putting the wrapping paper carefully to one side. His mother brought a big plastic trash bag to put the paper and boxes into, and he thanked each friend and neighbor with tears in his eyes.

"I thought I'd be all alone this birthday," he blubbered.

"Don't cry, man." Eric put an arm around his friend. "We're all here for you."

"Yeah, man, we miss you," Eric's twin brother said and ruffled Troy's hair. Scarlett plunked onto a black Naugahyde rocking chair in the next room, and put her feet up on a black storage ottoman which held a secret– a card inside that told Troy where a new red Schwinn wheelie bike with a banana seat was hidden in the basement, behind her workshop where he wouldn't have thought to look. Right beside the baseball glove and ball.

Rocker Patch hid under the couch. Scarlett left him there, glad he was safe from the antics of a houseful of preteens.

It was a birthday to remember!

Later, in his room, Troy's friends played with the Lego robots and the mechanical trains he had built. "Good job, Troy," said Paul Balakrishnan.

Troy laughed and stuck out his chest. One of the twins punched him in the stomach. He doubled over and whooshed air out of his open pink mouth then punched the boy back. They both grinned. Stevie Cardinal pushed him and they chased each other down the hall and back.

Troy stopped when one of the younger Cardinal girls came out of his room. They faced each other with a new recognition. Slowly, a smile eased over his face. She blushed and took his hand. "Happy birthday, Troy. You'll be a man soon, like my dad."

He hung onto her hand, both their faces glowing. Her hands were cool and soft. "You've grown up, Skye Cardinal. I didn't even notice until now," he stammered. "I see you almost every day, and I never noticed."

Then he pounded the girl on the shoulder. They both rushed back into his room to join their friends in more games.

In a corner of the room, Stevie was drinking a cola. "You have to get rid of that clown on your wall, man."

"Yeah," Troy replied, looking around his room. "This is a little kid's room."

Stevie took off his glasses and squinted at Troy. "Still see that light at night in your room?"

"Nah. Nothing scares me now. It was just some loser with a flashlight."

The parents began to arrive, one by one and two by two, to take their boys and girls home. Leela, Dorothy, and Karin stayed to help clean up. Exhausted, Scarlett fell into bed that night. She forgot to turn the light off in her room and was too tired to get up and do it. Troy tiptoed into her room later and turned off the light. "Goodnight, mom."

"Goodnight, son."

"I think we won't have to worry anymore, mom."

Scarlett sighed and turned over in bed. "I hope not, dear. Go to bed now."

34

The passing years were kind to them all. No lights winked on in Troy's room that he or his mom hadn't turned on. Neither did a tick-tock behind his walls disturb the silence of midnight. Their new "Touch-Tone" phone no longer trilled with a wrong number. Rocker Patch kept the mice at bay, or must have, because there was no scratching behind the walls. Only occasionally did the lights flicker and then after a thunderstorm, when John Aguila from the corner store would arrive with chocolate milk and sweets.

John remained a good friend to Charles, Scarlett, and Troy. He married late in life, after his mother died. Rocker Patch slept as usual with Troy in their house in Calder, in the boy's newly decorated bedroom with the movie posters, his General Electric boombox, and the Atari 2600 Charles gave him for Christmas that year. Scarlett said Charles spoiled him.

New Year's Eve, 1982:

Nancy and her son Scott Clarke sat with the television turned to *Happy Days* in their house which sported new aluminum siding, and welcomed their old friends with iced tea and pretzels. Angus couldn't contain his excitement at seeing his old friends. Blue-feathered Max sang and mimicked the intoxicating voices.

"I made a surprise for you all," Troy exclaimed. "To welcome the new year! Dad helped me with it. Or rather, Uncle Charles."

"We're all together now," Nancy smacked her hand on the verdigris country style kitchen table. Scarlett admired the split-oak baskets and used glazed ceramic tiles and canisters. Divorce had been kind to Nancy. Her spirit had returned and with it a flair for home decorating.

To Charles, who stood twisting his new gold wedding ring, Nancy said, "Our souls are at rest. Congratulations, Charles, and thank you. I know you had a lot to do with it. Now let's watch the ball drop in Times Square."

Angus woofed and rubbed his muzzle into Scarlett's hand. She stroked his silky ears and rubbed his chin. The parakeet sang "Charles, Charles," and Scott declared, "I taught him that, Troy."

Troy grinned crookedly and beamed. "Neat."

"A drink to celebrate?" asked Nancy.

"No, thanks," Scarlett replied. "I don't drink."

Troy, now thirteen, tall and lean like his parents, glanced at the metal and glass watch on his wrist. "It's time," he said. "Midnight." The little bird robot he had constructed sprang out of the watch face and exploded into his palm in a heap of gears, steel feathers, and springs. He laughed. "Rust in peace," he exclaimed. "Ruined the surprise!"

Charles put his manly arms around his new wife and bent her backward with the passion and tenderness of their first kiss of the new year. Troy hugged Nancy and Scott. Nancy's hazel eyes brimmed with tears.

"You look an awful lot like your uncle," Nancy said to him. "Don't you?"

Troy grinned.

"Nobody's perfect," said Charles. "Happy new year."

Scarlett giggled like a young girl. Throughout the universe, her voice sounded like a thousand bells. Tinderstruck by its loveliness, Michael Joseph Kane in Paradise halted momentarily from his heavenly tasks and listened.

"I'm nuts and bolts about New York," Troy declared. "Especially Times Square."

The ball dropped.

In years to come, Troy imagined Rocker Patch with the warm orange stripes and the warm low thrum, and Angus – with his soft brown eyes and red bandanna – chasing his father across fields of wild clover in a wind-rushed landscape in Paradise. Like kittens, puppies, or children again, carefree and forever young and unscarred, they remained always in his heart. Indeed, they lived forever.

You might also like:
Blood Sister by Kenna McKinnon

To read the first chapter for free, head to:
https://www.nextchapter.pub/books/blood-sister

Dear reader,

We hope you enjoyed reading *Ascending*. Please take a moment to leave a review, even if it's a short one. Your opinion is important to us.

Discover more books by Kenna McKinnon at https://www.nextchapter.pub/authors/kenna-mckinnon

Want to know when one of our books is free or discounted? Join the newsletter at http://eepurl.com/bqqB3H

Best regards,
Kenna McKinnon and the Next Chapter Team

ACKNOWLEDGMENTS

My friend and Beta reader, Judith Hansen of Michigan, has unfailingly, loyally, and with love helped me through the edits and many drafts of *Ascending*.

Marlene O Byard of Washington, DC proposed very helpful suggestions for the crucial first page.

To Miika and Petteri, my publishers at *Next Chapter*, who believed in me and this novel of love and final redemption. And to Bob, may he rest in peace. I love you.

Biography:

Kenna McKinnon is a Canadian freelance writer, author of *SpaceHive*; *Bigfoot Boy: Lost on Earth*; *Benjamin and Rumblechum, The Insanity Machine*; *Blood Sister; Short Circuit and Other Geek Stories; DISCOVERY: A Collection of Poetry*; *Den of Dark Angels; Engaging the Dragon;* and *Timothie Hill and the Cloak of Power*. Her most memorable years were spent at the University of Alberta, where she graduated with a degree in Anthropology. Kenna is a member of the Writers' Guild of Alberta and a professional member of the Canadian Authors Association. She has three children and three grandsons. Her hobbies include fitness, health, drawing, reading, walking, music, and entertaining friends. Writing is not a hobby; it is a childhood passion grown up!

Author's blog: http://KennaMcKinnonAuthor.com
Facebook: https://www.facebook.com/KennaMcKinnonAuthor
Twitter: http://www.twitter.com/KennaMcKinnon
Goodreads: http://www.goodreads.com/author/dashboard
LinkedIn: http://www.linkedin.com/in/kennamckinnon

Ascending
ISBN: 978-4-86752-502-9

Published by
Next Chapter
1-60-20 Minami-Otsuka
170-0005 Toshima-Ku, Tokyo
+818035793528

31st July 2021

Lightning Source UK Ltd.
Milton Keynes UK
UKHW010636090821
388558UK00002B/335